AF574636

THE GHOST BESIDE US

PETE NUSSWEILER WITH KRIS NUSSWEILER

Published by As We See It, a Division of Nunweiler Photography

For permissions, email:

pete-nunweiler@nunweilerphotography.com

Visit the author's website at www.petenunweiler.com

First Edition

ISBN 978-1-5323-7437-1

Cover design by Rob Williams, Designer

I Love My Cover

www.ilovemycover.com

Edited by Laura Wilkinson

"Conversations with Sara" used with permission from Kristi Lawrence.

Dedication

For Kris. You've had big shoes to fill as my biggest fan, but you believe in me every day and I will be forever grateful.

Chapter 1

As Always

"Sara?"

Alex jumped off the counter, but her expression showed more anxiety than it did excitement as she held her breath. She placed her hand on her heart with the anxiety thumping through her chest. She tried to regulate her breathing; a futile attempt to relax. She breathed short, rapid breaths through gritted teeth and held her left side as she felt a jolt of pain in her ribs from jumping off the counter. We both looked around for several moments, until she stared at me, awaiting my response. I rushed into the living room and turned off the music.

The chill faded and I slowly turned my head to the sides, looking for any visual signs of her. We listened without moving, breathing or even blinking our eyes. The only noise was the sizzling sound of bacon coming from the kitchen. Alex turned her gaze away from me and we both scanned the house without moving an inch.

Both of us snapped our heads towards the basement, wide-eyed. There was a heart-dropping noise through the closed door. It sounded like something falling off a shelf and striking several other things on its descent until it settled on the floor.

Alex walked next to me on my left side and whispered, "Oh, God, Toby, is it him?"

I matched her tone, "I sure as hell hope not."

I put my arm around her and she flinched from the ache in her ribs. I pulled my hand away and whispered, "Sorry." She nodded her head.

"Get the dowsing rods."

She tiptoed into the bedroom and brought the box to the dining room and set it on the table before carefully reaching into the box for the brass rods.

CLANG

The edge of one rod caught the edge of the box and dropped onto the table. My chest pounded, and I exhaled. We stayed still, looking around with only our eyes.

Creeeeak

I turned my head to her.

"That was me—sorry."

After a few minutes of calm, I walked to the stove, turned the bacon in the pan and turned the heat down on the burner. I pushed the eggs around the pan, scrambling them, but still trying not to make any more sound than necessary. Alex continued to search around. She paced the house, looking into open doorways. She spoke from a distance, but I couldn't make out what she said over the sizzling eggs in the pan.

I raised my voice; barely above a whisper, "What?"

She walked closer, "I said I don't like it. I feel like I'm being watched."

After looking around suspiciously again, I said, "I know. I feel it, too."

She walked over and leaned on the counter next to the stove. I glanced over at her when I noticed she was staring at me, expressionless.

"What is it, Alex? What are you thinking about?"

"Do you think he'll come back?"

I dropped the entire spatula into the pan, took a deep breath and looked up at the ceiling. I shook my head and she touched my arm. Flashbacks of that day flooded my thoughts in an instant. The most prominent memory was his strength. He was an unseen entity who threw me around the house like a couch pillow. He engulfed the entire house with blackness on a bright afternoon, and to top it off, he was thoroughly crazy. I've never been as afraid as I was that day. My heart raced as my memory replayed the twisted notes of the Jack-in-the-box.

"Well?" she urged.

I exhaled hard, looked at her and said, "I don't know, Alex. Let's hope not," then I pulled the spatula out of the pan with the tips of my fingers. I pulled a paper towel off the roll to wipe the handle of the plastic turner.

"Toby, what if he does?"

"Alex," I said with a hint of frustration. "I enjoy this stuff as a hobby, it's not like I'm professional or anything."

I turned my attention back to the frying pan and she put her arms around me and onto my chest from behind, placed the side of her head between my shoulder blades and said, "I'm sorry. It's just that you know more about this stuff than I do."

"I'm sorry too."

She leaned around me to look at my face and said, "Will you teach me more? I want to understand."

I murmured, listening for additional disturbances in the house, "First rule, and you can *never* break this; never—summon—anything. You don't have control over what you're bringing back. If you sense an entity, communicate with it. Figure out whether it's harmful or not."

"How do you know? Do you just ask?"

"You'll sense it. I can't explain it, but you'll sense it. Like now; we feel like we're being watched—we probably are. What worries me is—who's watching us? I've been to a lot of places where I sensed someone was watching me. As uneasy as it is, sometimes, it's not a big deal and it doesn't mean you're surrounded by evil. Hell, it doesn't mean there's anything there at all."

She leaned into me again and whispered, "Do you think something is here with us now?"

I turned my torso away from the stove and looked around. "What do you think?"

"It feels like it to me."

I turned back toward her, "Yeah, me too."

I scrambled the eggs more and continued, "The second rule is, don't assume every strange thing that happens, or feeling you get, is an entity in the house. Lights flicker and floors creak. Generally, there's an explanation. If there is, try to believe it's something rational and don't assume that it's paranormal."

I finished cooking breakfast and got plates and glasses out of the cabinet, utensils out of the drawer and orange juice out of the stainless-steel refrigerator and set them all on the counter. Alex kept looking around the house for any sign of Sara and reached for the half-gallon of orange juice. I gently slapped her hand to lighten the mood. She pulled it away with a jerk and looked at me with a smile and a disgusted, "UH!"

"Go sit," I said, grinning. "I've got this."

"Now who's being sassy, Mister?"

"That would be me, Miss Reagan. I learned from the best."

She sat down at the dining room table with a grimace. I carried the eggs over and served her from the pan. I put the bacon on a plate with paper towels to soak up the grease, put the dishes back on the stove and sat down at the table across from her. Throughout breakfast, we looked around the house with paranoid, suspicious eyes.

I couldn't get the sound from the basement out of my mind. When we finished breakfast, I put the dishes in the sink and told Alex, "I'm going downstairs to see what made that noise."

She looked at me like I was crazy.

"I'm going with you," she said.

It was like a cliché scary movie. I was the guy who checked out a strange noise in the house while telling the girl not to tag along, but has to run back when she gets attacked by something while he's not there to save her.

"Okay, come on," I said.

"Should I get the rods?"

"No, I just want to know what fell."

She held on to my arm as we crept along the galley kitchen, past the stone wall and stopped at the closed basement door.

"I still feel it," she said.

"I do too, Alex."

With my ear pressed to the small gap in the door where it meets the doorframe, I listened. I turned my eyes towards the door. Alex whispered, "Do you hear anything?"

I placed my finger up to my mouth and closed my eyes to focus all of my attention on listening to anything that might be behind the door or down the stairs. Hearing nothing, I whispered to Alex, "Ready?"

She nodded her head, so I grabbed the knob with my entire hand and turned it slowly. We were so silent, I heard the springs inside the door latch tighten. When the knob wouldn't turn anymore, I inched the door towards me with my eye centered on the opening. Nothing was breaking the light coming through. The door popped. I flinched. Alex tightened her grip on my arm.

When I pulled the door the rest of the way, I still didn't step through.

"Sara? Are you down there?"

I shifted my weight and Alex let go of my arm when I reached my right foot down to the creaky first step and paused. I took another step, and another, one by one, until I reached the bottom of the stairs with Alex right behind me. When we stepped into the theater room, we looked around and everything was in its place. I looked along the long wall towards the bar and out the sliding glass door on the wall across from us.

"I don't see anything at all," I said aloud.

"Check the garage."

We walked the length of the room to the door into the garage. I paused before opening it, turned the knob the same way I did to the basement and reached my hand in to open the bay door.

Alex screamed, and I jumped when we saw a possum run around the front of my truck, out of the garage and into the woods across from the door. We caught our breath and looked around the narrow paths on each side of my Sorento. There was a quart-sized paint can on the floor by a rack against the wall.

I sighed and told Alex, "It must have been this that fell."

I put it back on the shelf and looked around to see if it chewed anything up before going back inside. I then walked into the basement, pressed the button to close the bay door and turned off the light

"I've had about enough excitement with noises in my house."

Alex laughed and said, "A damn possum." We shook our heads at ourselves until Alex blurted out, "What the hell was that?" and froze.

"I don't know, I didn't hear anything."

"It was like a hissing sound."

"Like a snake?"

"No, like a—I don't know, but not a damn snake."

There was a breathy sound; like a weak voice whispering, "Hhhhaaaasss."

"Jesus, what the hell is that?"

"Hhhaaalllaaasss," it whispered again.

I looked at Alex, confused.

"Hhhaaallleexssss."

"Sara, where are you?" Alex said.

"Alllexsss."

"I'm right here, Sara."

She took a deep breath, stood straighter, closed her eyes and turned her head to the ceiling when she shivered.

The voice became clear when it slowly repeated a whispered, "Alex."

Alex put her arms up to her opposing shoulders, rubbing them for warmth. I reached out to touch her arm. It was cold.

I recalled the events that happened in the house only a few weeks before; the darkness, the jack-in-the-box, and of course, Daryl. I stared at Alex's face with rage building up inside me, waiting for Alex to open her eyelids to reveal blacked out eyes. I grabbed both of Alex's cold upper arms and demanded, "Open your eyes."

She opened them but was still looking up towards the ceiling.

"LOOK AT ME!" I shouted.

Her beautiful hazel eyes fixed upon mine and she asked, "What's the matter, Toby?"

I shook my head, held her in my arms for a moment, relieved and said, "I thought he had you again."

The cold sensation faded, I dropped my shoulders and said, "I'm sorry I yelled."

"Where did she go?" Alex asked.

"I'm not sure, but I bet she's not far. She sounds like she's still weak."

Alex looked around the room, "Sara, where are you?"

I heard her breathy voice. She was close.

"I'm—right here—beside you."

Alex smiled when Sara finished, "As—always."

"Where have you been?"

She waited a full two minutes for a response, during which, she called out her name and asked if she was okay.

"It's so strange," she said.

"What is?"

"How did she get so weak when she's not—you know—I mean, she doesn't have a body to get tired and weak?"

"It *is* a little weird. I always thought their energy came from either us or electronics. Oh, or water." I said.

"Water?"

"Yes. Water is like a portal of energy for them."

Without a response, we walked back upstairs, through the galley kitchen and in front of the sink in the larger kitchen. I ran the water and rinsed the dishes before putting them in the dishwasher. She helped me clean up, and we sat on the front porch in the rocking chairs until early afternoon. Sometimes we engaged in conversation, while other times, we remained silent so we could enjoy the sounds of nature.

"As always," Alex said.

"What?"

"Sara said she's right beside me, as always. What do you think she means by 'always?'"

"I don't know. She's said that to me, too."

"She did? When?"

"A while ago; after she threw a glass across the room once."

"You never told me that," she exclaimed.

"Yeah, I was drilling her with questions about the night Daryl killed her. Some of your story made little sense."

"I'm sure. Do you still question it?"

"No, it makes sense now, but that day, I was pointing out the things that didn't, and it made her mad. She begged me to stop asking questions."

"She knew I lied, and she protected me."

"Did she do that a lot?"

"We supported each other to a fault, Toby."

"How is that possible?"

"Oh, it's possible. It didn't matter what it was. We supported each other's ideas, no matter how crazy they were and supported each other's bad decisions; publicly, anyway. Sara had no problem supporting me in front of others but would kick my ass behind closed doors."

She gazed towards the tree line in the front and towards the gravel road. "We would do anything for each other." She looked at me and clarified, "Anything."

"What were you like; you know, as sisters—when she was alive?"

Alex rocked forward and stood up. "That's a conversation for another day, Mister Miller. I need to go home. Tomorrow's Monday and I have a few appointments."

I stood up with her. We put the equipment in the box and back into the closet. She walked around and gathered her things. When finished, I walked her to the front door. She stopped before I reached the door and turned towards the dining room.

"Right here beside you—as always." She said under her breath, with a hint of sarcasm.

"What are you thinking, Alex?"

"Bye, Sara," she called out.

She stood, waiting for a response; a response that never came. She crossed her arms and shook her head, turned towards the door and quietly said, "Liar," as she walked out.

Chapter 2

Best Friends

She walked down the steps and unlocked her car doors. Before getting into her car, she turned and said, “Hey, what are you doing Wednesday?”

My heart sank. I sighed and wistfully said, “I’m not sure yet, why?”

“Uh, oh, what’s going on Wednesday? You look like you lost your best friend.”

"It's funny you say that," I said as I leaned my head against the door frame and sighed again. "Wednesday is mine and Anna's anniversary."

Her shoulders dropped with regret, "Oh, God, Toby, I'm so sorry. I didn't mean—"

"It's okay, really."

She put her head down, shamefully, and got into her car. As she drove away, she shook her head and looked at me regretfully, then continued down the lane to the dirt road and turned left behind the trees. Sara was on my mind when I was back inside. I walked over to the open basement door and was about to call out to her. I considered how she might have felt. She was weak, barely able to communicate. I didn't want her to feel like she was being treated like an attraction at an amusement park or a house pet that was required to come running back whenever I beckoned her.

"See you soon," I said.

I closed the basement door and walked to the refrigerator for a beer, but decided my emotions might have been calling for something a little stronger. I got the rum out and mixed it with ice and a soft drink, then turned on some music. To prepare myself for Wednesday, I chose the Porch Music playlist and turned to sit on the back patio. When I did, I saw a silver switch on the wall in the corner, by my recliner. I had seen it before but didn't know what it controlled. I switched it on and looked around the house, then off, then on as I looked for lights and listened for anything that might have powered on. It seemed to control nothing, so I turned it off again. I walked out to the back porch with thoughts of Anna on my mind. I imagined her smile and her beautiful face.

I stretched and looked all over the porch, seeing all the same things I've looked at since I moved back in—except—hmm, there were little speakers in the corners of the patio where the roof met the house.

"Hmm," I mumbled out loud. I squinted my eyes in thought trying to figure out how to turn them on. I turned to the sliding glass door, opened it and walked over to the little silver switch on the wall, turned it on again and went back outside to see if the speakers worked. Of course, the first song that played faded out, so I stood still with the glass door still ajar.

"HA!" I said when the next song played inside *and* through the little outdoor speakers. I got the remote and stood back in the doorway and tested the sound. As I increased the volume, the sound was clear for such little speakers, with the perfect balance of bass, mid tones, and treble. I pressed the 'volume down' button, placed the remote on the small table next to me, leaned back and rocked, looking out at the tree line; occasionally sipping my beverage.

We always celebrated our anniversary here, in the mountains. What would we do if she was still alive? Would we be here yet? Yeah, we would have left Thursday night, stayed in Corbin, Kentucky and drove the rest of the way in the morning. We always did. If this was a rental cabin, this would be our second full day here. We would have driven along the Motor Nature Trail several times by now and spent time out in Cades Cove. Evenings most often included sitting on the porch with music, talking about our day or planning a hike for the next day. Sometimes, we spent time in the hot tub. Oh, the hot tub. Ohh, the hot tub.

I looked over at my own hot tub and imagined us in it. Each with a beverage, enjoying the view of the mountains from cabin rentals that were much higher in elevation than my Forever House. We always kept the lights off to make sure the darkness hid us as the water splashed rhythmically to our motion. I smiled and shivered at the thought. *Oh, the hot tub.*

My phone vibrated on my hip.

"Hey, Alex."

"Toby, I don't even know where to start and I don't think 'sorry' covers what I'm feeling. If I could take it back, I would."

"Alex, please stop worrying about it. It wasn't intentional. I'm fine."

"I saw it in your eyes, Toby. I didn't mean to hurt you in any way."

"I'm not hurting—well, not because of you. Hey, what did you have in mind for Wednesday, anyway?"

"Don't worry about it, you do what you need to on Wednesday," she encouraged.

"I will, but that might include you."

"Me? I don't think I'm comfortable being included in your anniversary plans."

"If not you, it will be a party of one. Really, I have no plans. Alex, I don't know what to do, how to feel, or how to spend my time. How do I live my life to fulfill my promise to her, yet take the time to remember to keep my promise to myself? Alex, you're all I have here

—I know I'm asking a shitty thing of you. I don't want to disrespect you, but for this, and for now, I need my friend. Will you help? Help me learn to live. Together."

She remained silent for a few seconds before answering, "Of course, I will. What do you have in mind?"

"Absolutely nothing," I said.

"How about this; let's take the day to remember. Tell me more about her. I'd love to learn more about her, anyway. We'll do the same things you did together and if it's too much, we can do something else."

"Are you sure you're okay with that? I mean, I'm asking you to support me through a day that's going to suck."

"I'll be whatever you need me to be, Toby. You said you need your friend. I'll be there. If you need your girlfriend, say the word, but we're in this together, like you said."

She was sincere. I hated asking her to help me get through a day that would be full of sadness, thinking of my widower, but I had no one else.

"Why don't you start by telling me how you spent your anniversary down here."

"We used to sit around the night before and try to plan the perfect day together. We were always in the park all day. I think, one year, we hiked to Abrams Falls, other years, we drove to different places without hiking at all. If we wanted to get out, we did. Sometimes, we followed the plans we made the previous night and other times, we didn't."

"Why don't I come over Tuesday night, okay? You can tell me how you want to spend Wednesday and we'll take it from there."

"I like that idea."

I was in my recliner when Alex got to my place around 8:30 on Tuesday night. I had spent the rest of Sunday and most of Monday writing and looking at old photos I had taken to see if any were good enough to post on my website. I only left the house once on Monday to go to the store for one item that I placed on the granite counter. It was the only thing on the curved countertop separating the kitchen and the dining room.

She took her bag into the same spare bedroom she stayed in the first night she stayed with me. When she came out, she must have noticed the puzzled expression I had on my face.

She smiled and said, "You said you need a friend. I'll be whoever you want me to be."

I was in a silly mood, so without hesitating, I said, "Ooh, how about a French maid that came in to clean and unexpectedly saw the homeowner sleeping on his bed—naked?"

"Ok, I won't be that," she laughed, and said more seriously, "How are you?"

"I'm okay. I got a lot of writing in over the last couple of days."

"Oh, good. Are you happy with it?"

"Yeah. I need to go back through it. I only have the first draft written out, but I'm happy with what I've got."

"Do you have any of that lemonade made up?"

"It's in the fridge. Help yourself."

I watched her as she navigated the kitchen cabinets to get a glass for her lemonade.

"Did you come up with any ideas for tomorrow?" she asked.

"I did."

She poured herself a drink and sat on the couch. "Really? What's the plan?"

"Let's start by getting breakfast in the morning."

"Okay, sounds like a great start. Then what?"

"Nothing. We'll leave the parking lot of the restaurant and figure it out from there. We can start by driving up around Morton's Overlook and Newfound Gap. We'll stop if we want, or keep going if we want."

She smiled and said, "That sounds perfect."

She looked around the house, "Any signs of my sister?"

I looked around, too. "No."

"Nothing at all?"

"Not since you were here."

"Toby," she said as she swirled the bit of lemonade at the bottom of her glass. "This lemonade should be illegal, it is so good. How do you make it?"

"It's quite complex, really. I start with a two-quart pitcher and fill it about halfway with water." She looked at me intently as I described the first step and drank the rest in one gulp before going back to the kitchen. "Then I pour the powder in the lid, all the way to the top; not that damn two-quart line just below the rim, I fill that sucker all the way to the top, dump it in the water, and stir the hell out of it." She was only slightly amused. I could tell by her smirk, combined with the shaking of her head back and forth. I laughed and finished, "Then I fill the rest of the pitcher with water and stir it again."

She poured more lemonade into her glass and walked around the counter to the single item I bought at the store the day before.

"Did you get a new candle?" she asked.

"I did."

She took the top off of it and held the lid up to her nose, "Oh, lavender, that's one of my favorites. Is that all you buy is lavender and peppermint? I noticed those are the only scents you have around the house."

"I have five peppermint and that one makes six of lavender."

She started back towards the couch and noticed my blank expression. "They're significant, aren't they?"

"One for each anniversary."

She smiled, "Do you ever light them?"

Tobias Miller, this is officer Sean Carter, your wife's been in an accident.

"Not in a while."

"Want to talk about it?" she asked.

"The last time I lit them was on March 10. I remember it like it happened yesterday. Anna was out with her friends for a girls' night out. I had a romantic evening planned for her when she got back. I talked to her on her way home, teasing her about not being too tired. You know, trying to build up anticipation. We hung up the phone and I ran around to make sure everything was perfect, from the candles to the chocolate fondue pot in the middle of the coffee table. The phone rang again."

Did you miss me that much, you had to call again?

"But it wasn't Anna. It was the police officer who saw her get hit."

"Oh, Toby, I'm so sorry."

She stood up, walked over and reached out for my hand. I took it and she led me out to the covered part of the porch and we sat in the rocking chairs.

"Tell me about Anna," she said.

"What?" I cleared my throat.

"You heard me. Tell me more about Anna. All I know is that you were crazy for each other, you loved the mountains, chased ghosts and, now, the little I know about her car accident."

My mind flickered with memories of my fourteen years with Anna and I wasn't able to pick out anything specific to share with her.

"Anna was—she was so—genuine, I guess is as good a word as any," I looked out at the yard beyond the screen room we sat in.

At the back of the yard, near the trail into the woods, I saw her standing, smiling at me with her long blonde hair and a light-colored summer dress with slits up both sides, almost up to her hips.

"Genuine? In what way?" Alex asked.

Anna's ghastly memory dissipated when Alex spoke.

"She was kind to everyone, never missing an opportunity to cast a smile to a friend or stranger. She was very structured and always had a Plan B in mind for everything. Hell, sometimes she had Plans C and D too."

"How did you meet her?"

Alex had never asked so much about Anna before, so I said, "Why do you want to know all this?"

"It's just conversation," she laughed. "To know *her* is to know more of you."

The memory played in my mind as I explained it.

"It was one of the few times I was at a bar. My friend, Ryan, and I were going through a divorce at the same time."

"You never told me you were married before."

"Yeah, I married my high school sweetheart. We had the world at our feet. Our world, anyway. We married when we were nineteen years old, so we felt like it was us against the world. It was for a long time, and we were good at it. There's a natural progression of life. People change at that age, you know? Still trying to figure out their own identity while trying to learn the other person's. It doesn't work out so well. As a young person, I was still trying to learn about myself. She and I talked a lot—and fought a lot. We didn't have the whole communication part figured out. We split up and got back together several times through the years."

"How long were you married to her?"

"Legally, ten years, but we split up five months before our tenth anniversary. When we first got married, people said we wouldn't make it ten years. It was almost a mission to prove everyone wrong. I was an angry person back then."

"What? Tobias Miller, I can't imagine you being angry for any reason."

My mind recalled yelling at her; blaming her. I remembered how she pushed me around sometimes and I remembered pushing her backwards into a pointed shelf when she got in my face once and her back struck the point.

"Ultimately, we didn't know how to disagree. Everything turned into a fight. We pushed each other around a few times."

I shook the thought from my mind, despising the person I once was.

"Alex, that was a different version of me I don't like to recall. I've worked hard not to be that guy ever again."

She placed her hand on mine and I looked at her, "Look, who you *are* defines you, not who you *were*. Forgive yourself for that and let it go."

I shook off the thoughts of that version of me.

"Anyway, Anna was different." I laughed and looked at her. "*I* was different. I think I needed my first marriage to fail to learn more about myself so I could learn how to have a healthy relationship. You know, we never got into a fight, me and Anna."

"Oh, come on. I'm calling bullshit on that one."

"Swear it. Don't get me wrong, we disagreed plenty of times, but we disagreed in a way that still respected each other's opinion. Few things in life are truly facts. Most things we believe in life are our own opinions and, the sooner I realized that, the sooner I could accept that a disagreement is simply a difference in opinion, not an 'I'm right and she's wrong' type of thing. I raised my voice once at Anna and we still laugh about it now." I looked out towards the yard. "Well, we *did* anyway. As I was trying to learn how to communicate better, she said something one morning that made me so mad. Instead of yelling and fighting, I reflected for *hours*, considering the best way to talk to her about it to let her know how she made me feel. I stressed over it long enough when I finally blurted out that she pissed me off that morning."

Alex opened her eyes in disbelief and asked, "What did she do?"

"She calmly walked into the room I was in and said, 'If you want to discuss this, I'll be glad to, but you don't get to talk to me like that,' and stood there, waiting for a response. I was ashamed of myself but proud of myself for working it out in my mind for two hours. I'm losing the point here—back to the night at the bar. Ryan and I were shooting pool and these two blonde girls walked up and placed quarters on the edge. We were so bold. We asked them if they wanted to play as teams and, to our surprise, they agreed. Things never happened that way for us. We had drinks and played for hours."

I continued to imagine it as I explained it to her. "It was her turn to shoot and she was at the corner of the pool table, opposite where I was and looked up at me with sensual eyes. I looked at her with a smirk and said, 'Don't look at me like that.' She kept staring at me, smiled and asked, 'Why not?' I smiled at her without responding. We went out on some dates and quickly became best friends."

"Did you ever meet her family?"

"No. She was adopted and—talk about dysfunctional. Anna was on her own at an early age. I think she looked for her birth family but got nowhere with it, so she stayed alone for a long time."

"On her own? What do you mean?"

"I don't know much about it. She didn't talk about it a lot."

"Hmm. It's interesting that she had a tough childhood and she turned out to be such a wonderful person." Alex said.

"She had no tolerance for people who used their past as an excuse for poor behavior. I suppose it's obvious why she felt that way."

"Is it getting any easier for you since her accident?"

"*Easy* is not a word I would use to describe it. It's living my life. It's time. It's the promise I made to Anna before she passed."

Alex sipped her lemonade, cleared her throat and said, "Did she *ever* talk about her childhood?"

"A bit here and there, but it was mainly insignificant memories from school or friends on the playground. I learned early in our relationship she didn't like talking about it. I mean, she never came out and said it, but when I asked questions, all I got were short answers. Hell, sometimes, they were short responses without answers at all. To be honest with you, Alex, she was so uncomfortable talking about it, it's making me uncomfortable now."

She placed her hand on my arm again, "Well, I certainly don't mean to pry. Will you tell me more about her accident?"

All of the events of the night in the hospital washed over me at once. The fear, the confusion, the loneliness, and the complete and total helplessness. It was overwhelming to think about all of it again. My heart raced as my blood pressure increased. I looked over at Alex and calmly said, "You know, I don't think I'm quite ready for that yet."

When I finished my beverage, I stood up and offered her more lemonade, which was more of a signal that the conversation was over.

"No, I still have half a cup."

"I'm going to get cleaned up. I'll be out in a little while."

I didn't want her to follow me. My life had been a roller coaster of emotions since the night of March 10 and it was starting to settle down a little. I undressed and entered the warm shower, standing under the water with my eyes closed.

"Want some company?"

"Anna! I need you now more than ever before."

"What's the matter, honey?"

"I'm doing the best I can here, babe. You told me to live my life and I'm trying, sweetheart. I'm really trying, but sometimes it's so hard to live without you."

"You have Alex now, and can't keep looking back. You kept your promise; till death do us part, remember?"

"But I'm not dead yet, Annaliese."

She smiled at me. Oh, how I missed that smile. I reached for her and she put her hand up. I stopped.

"Toby, you know I'm not real, right?"

"I know. Just because you're gone, doesn't mean I can't still talk to you and imagine you're here. You were always my voice of reason and I miss that."

She smiled bigger and said, "Does it help to pretend I'm here?"

"It does, yes, sometimes, anyway. Other times, it hurts all over again and I don't know what to do about that."

"Pain is real, Toby. Never deny yourself that, but don't stay hurt too long or the pain will define you. Now finish up and go to that beautiful girl out there. She needs you."

"I think we need each other, Anna."

She faded as slowly as the hot water did as the shower turned cooler.

Chapter 3

One Down

When I finished my shower, I put on pajama pants and returned to the porch, but Alex wasn't there. The only light outside was the fading sunset glow behind the distant mountains. The cicadas were deafening on that hot, summer night. I went back inside and called for Alex. She responded from the spare bedroom, "I'm in here." I stood in the doorway. She was on the bed, leaning on pillows with her phone in her hand.

"Whatcha doing?" I asked.

"Playing on my phone, but I'm going to lay down now. I ran through the shower while you were cleaning up, I hope you don't mind."

"Of course, not. You have everything you need?"

She looked around, "Yeah, I think so."

I walked next to the bed and leaned in to kiss her, "Goodnight."

She smiled, "Goodnight, Toby."

I turned off the light on the side table and walked through the house, into the master bedroom. With the doors open, I undressed before climbing into bed and reached out to turn the lights off. I had gotten used to the darkness since May, being away from street lights, but the darkness was still remarkable. I heard a distant click, then saw a glow coming from the other side of the house.

"Sorry," I called out. "I forgot you're not a fan of the dark."

"It's okay. Goodnight."

I got up, put my boxers on and walked through the living room to the doorway of the spare room. "I have night lights if that will help; that way, you don't have to have the big light on."

"Are you sure?" she asked.

I turned away before she even finished talking and called back, "I'm sure," then got three of the night lights from the kitchen drawers. One for the living room, one in the bathroom and one in the spare room with her. I turned off her main light again.

"You didn't have to do that, but thank you."

"It's nothing, really."

"Okay, goodnight."

"Goodnight, Alex."

About two minutes after I got back into bed, my phone vibrated. I reached over to see who had texted me. It was Alex.

TUESDAY, JUNE 26 10:16 PM

You Okay?

Yes, of course.

You?

Yeah, I'm fine. Just checking on you.

Thank you.

TUESDAY, JUNE 26 10:20 PM

This is a little weird.

I guess it sort of is, isn't it?

LOL! Yes, it is.

TUESDAY, JUNE 26 10:24 PM

Want to come over?

I heard her laughing from across the house before she called out, "Yes."

She walked in carrying one of the night lights and two pillows, reached down to an outlet to plug in the night light, and jumped into bed on my right side. She shivered.

"You're shivering, is it—"

"No, just cold. The air conditioner was blowing right on me."

She laid facing me, pulled her hands up to her chest and leaned her head against mine with my arm around her back. While I rubbed her arm with my fingertips, she made circles on my chest with hers.

I woke up at first light with Alex laying against my back and her arm around me. I pulled her hand up to kiss it gently and stared out the sliding glass door when a rush of thoughts hit me.

To not wake Alex, I got out of bed slowly, put my pajama pants on and walked out to the covered patio by the hot tub. I recalled the events of the years before when Anna and I started every anniversary morning with a cup of coffee, watching the sunrise from a balcony at a high elevation. I fixed my eyes on my own backyard, blinking fast trying to fight back more tears.

"Happy anniversary, sweetheart."

I had my moment with Anna and composed myself before going back inside. I slid the glass door open to the master bedroom and stood in the doorway for a moment to watch Alex sleep. She looked so peaceful. I laid back down on the bed, facing her, and gently pushed her hair away from her face with a single finger. She smiled but didn't wake up.

Go to that beautiful girl out there. She needs you.

When all of her hair was behind her ear, I leaned over and kissed her forehead. She squinted her eyes as her breathing changed and she faded out of sleep. She smiled again, "Good morning," she said in a scratchy voice.

I whispered, "Get up, sleepy head. We have a lot to do today."

"Mmm," she mumbled with a bigger smile. "Happy Anniversary, you two crazies."

I chuckled, "Thanks."

She sat up, "You okay?"

"Yeah, I'm all right. I went outside and spent a few minutes alone with Anna a little while ago."

"The first year is the worst, Toby. The first anniversary, the first Christmas, your birthday, hers. Is this the first significant date since she passed?"

"Yes, it is."

"Well, a wise man once told me, sometimes, things suck and you just have to let them. Toby—today is gonna suck."

"I expect that, but I don't want to *make* it that way. If it sucks at the end of the day, then it does."

I walked to the kitchen to make a pot of coffee and continued to talk to her, "I don't think I want to do all the same things today that Anna and I did. That's living backwards, not forward. I deserve new memories and I think she'd want it that way."

"So, how are we starting our day?" she called out from the bedroom.

"Oh, we're still getting breakfast, but we need to get ready and leave soon. I don't want to waste the day away."

Her voice was scratchy with a touch of a sassy whine as she got out of bed, "Okay, boss man, I'm up—I'm up."

Once we dressed, I gathered the camera equipment, filled the cooler with drinks and loaded the Sorento. Alex prepared coffee in two travel mugs. "Is that everything?" she asked.

"I believe so."

We drove towards Gatlinburg in thoughtful silence. She turned and asked, "What's on your mind, like, right now?"

My mind was all over the place, but I focused on what I was thinking at the moment she asked, "How the hell can I not know anything about Anna's childhood?" I said.

"What?"

"You were asking questions yesterday, and I didn't have answers. How could I have been so close to her and know nothing of her childhood?"

"Everybody has secrets, Toby. It's not always because people don't want to share. Sometimes, it's because they don't know how to say it or because the memory is too painful. It's nothing to beat yourself up about."

I sighed. "Maybe you're right, but that doesn't help right now. I should have known. If it *was* that painful, I should have been her safe place so she could tell me."

"I'm sure she would have told you in time—where are we going?"

The sun was beaming through the windshield as I drove Southwest towards town and the temperature climbed. "We're going to that little shop near Stoplight Ten to get a breakfast sandwich." I glanced over and she was fidgeting with her phone. "And what are you thinking right now?"

She stared at me for a moment, then looked back and forth between me and her phone without responding at all.

I laughed, "Wow, that's a lot. How do you think of it all at once?"

"Shut up, Tobias," she laughed, then answered, "Not a whole lot, I guess. I'm showing a house on Thursday. It's down by the river. My clients want this house so badly."

"They going to put in an offer?"

"I'm pretty sure they will. They're not asking anything ridiculous; only four thousand below asking price. I mean, that should be attractive to the sellers, for sure."

We made small talk the rest of the way until we reached our first stop and put in our order. As they prepared our food, we looked around the shop at the souvenirs, like I had done with Anna so many times. I read the funny signs on the carousel rack, picked up shot glasses and placed them back on the shelves at least a dozen times, getting lost in the moment. Over by the coffee mugs, I saw a unique design I hadn't seen before. I smiled, turned around and said, "Hey, babe—" but Anna wasn't there. Alex was nearby and responded, "Yeah, what's up?" I handed her the mug as if I called her, but it wasn't my intention. She laughed at the saying and gave it back. I put the mug back on the shelf as they called my name to pick up our order. I turned back towards the souvenirs and watched the ghosts of the past as mine called out to Anna's, "Our order's ready."

When they both looked up at me, I turned away.

When we got our order, we drove up the mountain and pulled off at Morton's Overlook; a place that offered a heavenly view of the mountains to the West. I put the SUV in park and asked Alex, "Do you mind if I take a moment?"

"You okay?"

"Yeah, give me a few minutes, if you don't mind. I promise I won't do this all day."

I got out of the truck and sat on the opposite side of the stone wall, facing the magnificent display of nature. There were few others in the pull-off so I felt like the beautiful scene was created just for me.

To my right and to my left was a spur, and straight out was a clear view of The Chimney Tops a few miles away in a distance. It was quiet, other than the occasional sound of a bird chirping or car driving further up the mountain to Newfound Gap. The sun was rising over the high mountain behind me, casting perfect light on the draw straight in front of me that led to town. At five thousand feet in elevation, it was much cooler than it was in Gatlinburg. The smell of mountain air was strong with a slight breeze fluttering through the surrounding trees.

I closed my eyes and inhaled to engage all of my senses, then opened them slowly. My thoughts began with my lovely Anna and I smiled.

"Anna," I whispered when I confirmed no one could hear me. "how many times do you think we've been here? I bet it's close to fifty. I can't count the number of sunsets we watched here; each of us with our cameras set on tripods." I looked around again. "It sure isn't the same without you. Independence Day is coming soon. I've been thinking of the time we were at the midnight parade a few years ago."

I laughed out loud but also tried to keep quiet. Tears welled up in my eyes, but not from sadness.

"Remember our shock that night? Oh my God, parents were throwing money into the street and the kids—"

It became difficult to talk because I was laughing so hard. I looked around to make sure I was still the only one there.

"The fucking kids running around, picking up the coins like psycho little bastards, knocking each other over for the penny that rolled in a ten-foot circle. We stared at each other and you said, 'Talk about feeding the greed.' We were lost for words. You kept saying how unbelievable it was and that it was the perfect example of so many problems with today's kids and our society. I mean, it wasn't funny at the time. It was rather sickening, but looking back on it—man, that was funny stuff."

I took a few deep breaths to control my laughter. My smile faded.

"What do I do, babe?"

I heard her voice in my head.

> *"Toby, sweetheart, I can't imagine how difficult it must be for you, but think of this; and only this. Are you truly living? You want to be an author, but you don't write much. You want to be a photographer, but you've only been out once. You have a beautiful home. It's perfect. Don't lose sight of your dreams; not for me, and not for Alex. So, are you truly living? I can't answer that, sweetheart; only you can."*

My mind shifted to Alex.

She's beautiful, she's smart, she's fun, she's sassy as hell and she's as lost as I am. I didn't seek her out. It just happened. I think she's more comfortable with our relationship than I am—but why? Am I afraid? Am I holding on too tightly to the memories of once upon a time?

"Scue me," I heard from behind me. I turned to see an Asian man smiling as he approached.

"Yes?" I replied.

"You take pitchure?"

He nodded his head fast as his family followed.

"Sure," I said as I pulled my legs to the other side of the wall and walked towards him. He handed me his camera and spoke to his family in his native language. They stood in front of the wall, smiling, with the valley behind them. I took a few pictures, returned his camera and asked, "Is that okay?"

"Yeah, yeah," he said, nodding without looking at the photos.

There were several more cars in the pull-off. I called out to Alex to have her join me. We walked over to the wall once again and looked out towards the valley. We stood, hand-in-hand. She rested her head on my shoulder as we took in the scene. I put my arm around her, pulled her closer and looked into her eyes. I kissed her once, and we looked back out at the heavenly view. Being there, with Alex, was like gazing out at the breathtaking landscape for the very first time.

We got into the Sorento and drove further up the mountain, where we ate our breakfast sandwiches at Newfound Gap. We chose a parking space near the sign for the Tennessee and North Carolina State Line, facing East, into the sunrise. When we finished, we drove back down the windy mountain road. After we passed the trailhead for the Chimney Tops, I saw a sign on the left side of the road with a pull-off just big enough for one vehicle; QUIET WALKWAY. I crossed over the double yellow line and braked hard to stop in the pull-off.

"What's the matter?" Alex blurted out.

"Not a thing," I said with a smile.

I turned off the truck and said, "Come on. We're going for a hike." When we got out, we looked around at the lush green of the Smoky Mountains and the small opening into the woods.

"Is this another old favorite of yours?" she asked.

"Nope. I've never been here." She smiled at me. "Anna and I used to talk about checking out these little quiet walkways, but never took them. Maybe once out towards Cades Cove." We stepped across the grass and onto the dirt trail. "Now, the quiet walkways will be *our* thing."

"Create new memories in familiar places."

"Right."

As we walked along the narrow trail, holding hands, Alex said, "So, we'll have a thing? I like it. Hmm, you have a thing."

I chuckled, "You like my thing."

She shifted her weight, pushing her shoulder into mine, and knocked me off balance, but I caught myself on a nearby tree before falling. The trail led us to a small cascade. The sun was sparkling off the tiny creek.

Alex said, "You should have got your camera out of the truck."

"I don't need it. I'll capture everything I need in here," I said and tapped the side of my head.

We spent the rest of the day in the park, stopping at random pull-offs and bantering back and forth about whatever came to mind.

We drove around the Cades Cove loop and were on our way back, enjoying the park—until traffic stopped along the winding river road somewhere between Tremont and the Metcalf Bottoms picnic area.

"Bear jam?" I asked.

"Bear jam?" she laughed. "What's a bear jam?"

"When all the tourists stop driving in the middle of the road when they see a bear."

We stretched our necks and swayed back and forth, trying to see around the vehicles in front of us, inching along at half a car length at a time with few cars traveling the other direction.

"Will you open your window, please?" she asked.

"Sure."

When I did, she leaned back and closed her eyes, "I love listening to the water."

"Open yours, too," I said. "You'll hear the echo off the rock wall."

We listened to the water as I inched the car forward. We moved far enough to see a bend in the road and several people out of their cars looking down into the river.

"I bet you're right," she said. "There's probably a bear down in the river."

I hesitated before I said with earnest, "It's not a bear."

Alex stretched to look around the vehicles again, "What is it?"

"It's a young couple. They drove off the road at the bend—they didn't make it."

"How do you know?"

"Because I can see them."

"Toby, you're scaring me."

"Try being me for a while. I don't like this any more than you do," I said as I placed my hand on hers.

She bit her fingernails, trying to look away but still glancing forward occasionally. "What are they doing?"

"He's yelling at her; pointing his finger in her face and blaming her. She's crying. Every time she tries to talk, he yells again to silence her."

"And you can actually see them?"

"Yes."

"Is there something you can do?"

"Like what? Walk up there and yell at the man that nobody else can see?"

"Okay, so maybe not," she said.

Neither Alex nor I spoke as we neared the ninety-degree bend to the right. I watched them; he was still yelling and she was still crying. I looked in my mirrors to make sure no one else could hear. When I confirmed it was clear, I said out the opened window, "Lighten up on her, man. It's not her fault. Why don't you go down the hill and look inside your car?"

They both turned their heads down the bank at their car as traffic broke free in front of us. A park ranger was approaching on the opposite side of the shoulder as I sped up. I glanced into my side mirror. The young man had his hands on his head in shock, and the young lady dropped to the ground.

"They were right there?" Alex asked while looking out the windshield.

"Yes."

"Did he respond to you?"

"They looked into their car. They know what happened now."

We drove the rest of the way home in silence. The sun had set behind the mountain by the time we got through Gatlinburg.

We pulled into the garage, unloaded the truck and put our pajamas on. I put on long, cotton bottoms, and she wore a long t-shirt and we sat on the back porch.

"This last week has been insane." I said. "Look how tall the damn grass is already. Didn't I just cut it?"

"I think you did over a week ago, and it's rained since then."

"Weird."

"What's weird, Toby?"

"I think you're right."

"Don't be an ass all your life, Toby?"

"Oh, come on, please? Just for—"

I stopped when I flashed back to the last phone conversation I had with Anna when we exchanged the same words.

"What is it?" Alex asked.

"Nothing."

She gave me that look again, so I clarified, "During my last phone conversation with Anna, I said something to her and she replied with the same thing." I smiled. "Don't be an ass all your life, Toby."

"I'm sorry."

"No, it's okay. I guess this is part of learning to live again."

"So, how was your anniversary, aside from that last little adventure by the bend?"

"The first is the hardest right?" She looked at me without responding. "It really wasn't all that bad. I had my moments, but it didn't suck as bad as I thought it would." I looked straight at her and said, "I thank you for that, Alex."

She said nothing, so I finished, "One down. We still in it together?"

Her hazel eyes smiled at me and her brunette hair draped over her right shoulder. "Of course, we are."

Chapter 4

In Time

"Hope you don't mind me asking," she prefaced. "What was your wedding day like?"

"Oh my God, it was hot. I mean, like *hot,* hot. Our ceremony was at 9:00 in the morning and it was already ninety-two degrees. As bad as it was for us, it was going to be worse for another couple. Somebody was getting married at the same place at 2:00 in the afternoon. It was so humid and we stood for so long, I had sweat dripping down my legs."

Another memory flashed into my mind. "The morning was beautiful. We got up and stood on the porch of our cabin soon after first light. There was a bird sitting on a wire just off the wooden deck and a few feet above us singing a distinct song that was a combination between a whistle and a chirp. We stood there, watching him for a while, and heard a noise in the tree line across a little grassy access road next to us. It got our attention, and we watched as a fawn stepped out of the woods."

"Awe."

"She was beautiful. It was amazing. We watched her for a while and she trusted us enough to take a couple steps closer. We observed that deer for every bit of 5 minutes before it ran off. The bird was singing the entire time. I actually have some video of that morning down in the basement."

"Really? You thought to get your camera out?"

"I carried that camera everywhere with me. It was always ready to capture something. I used to make family videos for Christmas every year. It was our way of sharing our little world with the rest of the family and another little hobby of mine. I pieced together videos and photographs that are timed to music."

"You said you used to; why did you stop?"

"I haven't put together a video since the year Mom died. I couldn't do it."

She shook her head back and forth and mumbled, "Where have you been all my life?" I don't think she expected an answer. "Is there anything you can't do, Mister?"

"Refinish furniture—well, I *can* do it. I did it once."

I looked out towards the yard without fixing my gaze on anything specific before I finished with, "But I really didn't like it. It's messy and a lot of work."

"Can I watch your videos sometime?"

"Yeah, I don't mind. Personally, I'm not ready for that yet, but you're welcome to watch them whenever you want."

I thought about all of our conversations since Tuesday; how I got frustrated with all the questions about Anna's childhood. She was never that inquisitive. Instead of allowing myself to get upset again, I expressed what was on my mind.

"You suddenly seem really interested in Anna. Why?"

She didn't look at me when she said, "No particular reason. I'm interested, that's all. Call it a girl thing."

My phone vibrated on my hip. I pulled it out of its case and got excited. "Oh!" I said as I fumbled to answer it.

"Ryan! What's up, buddy?"

"Not much, man. What are you up to?"

"Oh, not a lot, sitting outside with Alex."

"Alex?" he said with a mix of confusion and disgust.

I thought for a minute. I hadn't talked to him since I stayed with him the night before I left Indiana and tried to sneak out without having to say goodbye. He knew nothing about Alex.

"Oh, buddy. We have so much to catch up on."

Alex touched my arm and I turned to her. She mouthed, "You want me to go inside?"

I shook my head and mouthed, "No, you're fine."

Her sassy attitude showed itself when she moved her head from side to side and mouthed back, "Oh, well, thank you," with a mile-wide grin.

I tried not to laugh as I returned my focus to the phone call. Ryan had just finished saying something, but I wasn't paying attention so I asked him, "What's that, man? Sorry."

"Are you doing anything for the fourth?"

I pulled the phone from my mouth and asked Alex, "Hey, do we have any plans for the fourth?"

"Sure don't," she said.

I tilted the phone back to my mouth, "No, man, nothing here, why? What's up?"

There was silence on the line. I looked at the top of my phone to confirm the signal. I had perfect reception, so I returned it to my ear.

"Ryan? Did I lose you?"

He was defiant when he said, "No, man. Who's Alex?"

"It's a long story, but she's my—lady friend." I looked over at Alex and she grinned.

"So soon?"

"Ryan, if you've ever trusted me before, I need you to trust me now. Like I said, it's a long story."

"You okay?" he asked.

"I am. Really," I assured him.

"Look, man—if you're okay, I'm okay. Just seems kind of fast."

"Tell me about it. What are *you* doing for the fourth?"

"Well, that's what I'm calling about. Me and Shanna figured we might come visit you. I read somewhere that there's a midnight parade in Gatlinburg the night of the third."

"That would be awesome, man. I have plenty of room. I found the perfect home that Anna and I used to talk about. Remember, we dreamed about our Forever House?"

"Yeah, I remember."

"Wait until you see it. It's a three-bedroom on seven acres of property."

"Did you say a three-bedroom?"

"Yes."

"Good, because we've already talked to Jake and Melissa; they're in."

"No kidding? That will be so awesome to get together. When are you coming this way?"

"I'm thinking we'll come down on the second, so we have a full day before going to the midnight parade."

"Works for me. Stay as long as you'd like."

"Cool. You back to work yet?"

I hadn't thought about work since I texted my boss the morning after Anna died. I remembered him telling me to take as much time as I needed.

"No. As a matter of fact, I haven't thought about it until you just said it. Damn, I better call him."

"Yeah, that might be a good idea," he said through laughter. "Hey, one more thing. I know today's—you know."

"Yes, I know."

"You're sure you're okay?"

"I'm fine, dude. Really."

"Well, for what it's worth, Happy Anniversary."

"That means a lot, pal. Thank you."

"What's your address?"

I gave him my address and he told me he'd be in touch as it got closer, then we ended the call.

I turned to Alex, "Wow, I can't remember the last time I got a phone call that wasn't you."

"That's kind of sad, Toby. Nobody calls you?"

"Not really. Want to go inside?"

"Sure."

She stood up and stretched her shirt down. We walked into the house and sat on the couch, facing each other.

"I have to say, that was one of the strangest experiences of my life this afternoon," I said as I casually started rubbing her leg, below the knee.

"I want to know how you can see them."

My phone vibrated again. "I guess nobody calls me except for tonight. Was there some alert that told the world to call Toby Miller today—Hello?"

"Toby, it's Sam Hunt, how are you?"

"Wow, I'm good, Sam. How are you?"

I held the phone with one hand and kept rubbing her leg lightly with my other.

"I finally got the house sold for you. We can close as early as Friday."

Surprised, I said, "Friday? Like, the day after tomorrow, Friday?"

"Is that too soon? I can push it out to next week, but with the holiday, it may delay until the following week."

"No, Friday is fine. I'm guessing I need to be there to sign, right?"

"Yes, this part we can't do electronically. How does 2:00 sound to you?" he proposed.

I calculated the drive in my mind and backed into a leaving time of 6:00 AM

"2:00 should work. Thanks, Sam. I appreciate all you've done." I was about to end the call, but suddenly, I thought of something important. "Oh, how much did it sell for?"

"Five thousand under list, is that okay?"

"We agreed I'd go down by six, so five under is great."

"Good." He paused and said, "Toby?"

"Yeah, Sam."

He dropped his voice and asked from the heart, "How are you?"

"I'm doing okay. As good as one can ask for, anyway."

"That's good. We've known each other a long time and I think of you often."

"Thanks, man, I appreciate it."

I hung up the phone and told Alex, "I'm closing on my house on Friday."

"I gathered that from the conversation. Congratulations. You got good equity in the home?"

"Yeah—all of it."

"No shit?"

"None at all. I paid off the house at the end of April when I got the insurance check from Anna."

"Jesus, Toby, and there was still enough to buy this one outright?"

"And live off of for a while. I am glad the house sold though."

"I'm sure it's a relief. Did your realtor do everything for you?"

"Yeah, I've known him since we were teenagers. He told me to let him know when I got all my stuff out and he'd take care of the rest."

"That's great, Toby." She leaned back and sighed. It wasn't until then I realized that my hand had made its way above her knees and I was making circles on her leg with my fingertips. Her other leg was still off the couch with her foot on the floor. I kept rubbing as I continued, "Anyway, as far as this afternoon—I wish I knew how I can see them too."

We continued the conversation, but I'm not so sure what else we talked about. I focused on what I was doing to her leg, eventually, working my way back down her leg to give her a foot massage. When I finished one foot, I tapped it and reached for her other leg. She sat, facing me with her feet on the couch in front of her and I rubbed both of her legs, starting at her calf, and gradually inched my way up to her knees again. I didn't know how it was affecting *her*, but *my* heart was beating a little stronger and faster as I moved my hand higher up her thigh. The tip of the middle finger on my right hand felt something. It was smooth. My God, the thirty minutes of attention on her legs aroused her. I looked into her eyes. She seemed embarrassed at first, then blurted out, "See what you do to me, just from rubbing my legs?"

There was an intensity in my eyes when I put both of my hands on her knees and pushed them apart, then shifted my body so I was lying on the couch facing her. She grabbed my head at the same time she threw hers backwards, looking up at the ceiling and tensing up her entire body in a blissful release.

A half hour later, when we stood up, her legs shook as she walked towards the spare bathroom. I heard the shower come on and considered my options. I waited until I heard breaks in the water hitting the tile floor and joined her. We washed each other sensually and stayed in the shower with both of her hands inching down the cool tile walls until both of our legs were shaking and weak.

"I have *got* to get a bigger water heater," I said as we shivered with towels wrapped around us.

Thursday morning, we watched the sunrise with coffee in the hot tub. When it became bright enough to see, we watched my neighborly bear with her three cubs come out of the woods at the four-wheeler trail; a peaceful scene that increased my appreciation for the Forever House even more.

When we finished in the hot tub, Alex asked, "Hey, do you mind if I use your computer for a little while? I have things I need to check on and it will be much easier on the computer than on my phone."

"Sure, I don't mind. Use it any time you want. You don't have to explain."

"Okay, thank you."

While she did her research, I cleaned all of my camera equipment so it was ready for the next photo shoot, then I put away everything else from the day before, except for the small cooler.

"I better go home so you can get ready for your trip tomorrow," she said after getting dressed and gathering her things. "Know when you'll be back?"

"I'll probably just go to closing and come back home after."

"You're not going to see your friends?"

"They'll be here next week; I'm not worried about it."

"Don't be stupid, Tobias. If you get too tired, don't be a hero. That's fourteen hours of driving for an hour-long appointment."

I put my head down and said, "Yes, ma'am."

She shook her finger at me and said, "Damn right," and hugged me. She pulled away, looked into my eyes and said, "I love you, Toby."

I smiled at her, kissed her and said, "Thank you so much for yesterday."

She looked deeper into my eyes. "In time, Toby; in time. And you're welcome. Let me know when you're on your way back please."

"I will. I promise."

She looked all around the house and said, "Wait, before I go, can I try something?"

"Sure."

Curious, I watched her walk into the bedroom. When she returned, she brought the box of equipment out, set it on the table, opened it and retrieved the dowsing rods.

"Remember, address only her," I said.

She nodded her head and stood in the middle of the living room with the brass rods pointing away from her until they stopped swaying.

"Sara?"

The rods crossed.

"What the hell, Toby! What does that mean?"

"It means yes, Alex; apart means no."

The rods slowly pointed straight again.

"So, it *is* you?"

They crossed again.

I called Sara's name, "Do you think you're strong enough to talk to us for a few minutes?"

The rods swayed a few times, began to cross, then separated before finally crossing definitively.

"Alex, turn the spirit box on."

She walked over to the table, turned the knob until it clicked and increased the volume of the static.

"Hi," we heard through the static.

"That's her?" Alex asked.

We heard her elegant tone, "Duh, Alexandra."

She looked over at the spirit box and laughed. "Really, you hussy? You're going to 'duh' me after all this time?"

Sara giggled, then said, "Not long."

"What do you mean?"

I answered for her, "She doesn't have the strength to talk for long."

"Are you hurt?" Alex asked.

"No—just weak—not long."

"How long does this last?" Alex asked me.

"The first time she talked without the equipment was the night I had to get you from the bar. That was—oh, wow. That was only hours after we communicated through the spirit box."

"Yes," we heard through the static.

Alex smiled with excitement, "Should we turn it off and wait so she gets even stronger?"

"No," Sara said.

Alex replied with, "Okay. You said you talked without equipment. What was the first thing you said?"

"Is—she okay?"

Alex turned with her hand on her mouth and spoke fast, "Oh, God, that was the night you undressed me and I still don't remember how I got to your place."

I laughed, "Yes, that's the night."

"Gentleman," we heard from the Spirit Box

"What do you mean, gentleman?" Alex asked.

"Toby—gentleman. Take care—when—I couldn't."

"Yes, you always took care of me."

"Baby—sister."

"Baby sister? By what? A few minutes? It was never your job to take care of me."

Sara's laughter faded into the static, "But I did."

"Yes, you did. I was the wild one. You were my voice of reason. You covered for me when I needed it and always kept my secrets."

Static—"Babysitter—" *Static*

"Oh, bullshit. You were my sister, not my damn babysitter, you liar," Alex laughed.

Her smile faded. We stared at the little box and listened to the white noise for what seemed like a full minute.

"Love you—Alexandra."

"I love you too, Seraphina. Will you stick around this time?"

The static faded without a response. She was sad when she turned off the spirit box and put the equipment back in the closet.

She walked back out to the living room and said with an artificial smile, "It's good to have her back."

"Is it?" I challenged.

"Why wouldn't it be?"

I took her hands in mine, looking deep into her eyes. "Alex, do you remember what I told you when you first found out she was here?"

"That you had talked to her several times and kept it from me?"

"Yes, that same conversation. You asked me why she's still here. Do you remember that?"

"Yes."

"Alex, I believe spirits and ghosts are the souls of people who have died."

"Obviously."

"To you, yes, but not to others. Some believe they're all demons. I think they're all here for some reason. Sometimes, they're here to protect us."

"Like angels?"

"Sure, that's as good a word as any. Others, I believe stay behind for a reason. A reason they chose."

Alex recalled, "She believes this is her Hell. Her punishment for not standing up for herself against Daryl."

"You do remember. So, I ask again, is it that good to have her back? I mean, for her sake."

I knew she understood when she turned her eyes away from me in thought. She sighed several times as I brushed her arm with my fingers. I had grown close to Sara, so the thought of her not being there was difficult for me too, and that was selfish.

She gathered her things again, turned towards the door and called out into the air, "Bye, Sissy. I love you." She looked around, waiting for a response.

"In time, Alex," I said. "In time."

Chapter 5

Road Trip

"You really love her, don't you?" I heard after Alex closed the door. I didn't respond, only looked around the house. "Why won't you say it?"

"Sara, the last time I said the words out loud was to my wife."

"Anna was a different person, Toby. What happened to her was tragic. The accident ripped her away from you, I get that, but as long as you're going to pursue my sister, I think it's time to let her know."

"She knows."

"I'm sure she can feel it, but a girl likes to hear it."

"I tell you, Sara, this is not the conversation I imagined we'd be having when you could talk again."

"I've *been* able to."

"What? Are you saying you're holding back? Not talking out loud by choice?"

After a full minute with no response, I went into the bedroom and laid out clothes for the next day, then refilled the cooler with water and soft drinks.

"Toby."

"What?" I snapped.

"She was here since Tuesday night and she didn't bother talking to me."

"Really? Don't you think that's a little petty based on—your situation?"

"And, neither did you, Toby. I'm here with you every day. I have never left your side since you got here. Were you only interested in me because I'm dead? My sister gets the rest of you now. Your attention, your touch, your heart; she gets it all."

I could hardly believe what I was hearing. "Where are you? Will you show yourself so we can talk properly?"

"I can see you just fine."

I sat in the recliner and contemplated how to respond to her, but nothing brilliant was coming to mind, "What are we going to do about that?"

"I don't know. I can't give you what you want without—"

"Without what?"

"Never mind. It's a bad idea."

"What is it?"

"Well, you don't get to hear it. I feel terrible even thinking it."

"Okay, I'll respect that."

"Toby, you know how I feel about you."

"Sara, I'm not sure I do. I can't work out when your actions were your own and when Daryl influenced them."

"Everything was me until I tried to let Alex know I was here. I don't remember much after that. I think I released him when the jack-in-the-box popped open. The little experiment on the couch; that was me. Telling you I had nothing to give; that was me."

I jumped in when she paused, "And laying with me the night of the storm?"

"What are you talking about?" she said, confused.

I remembered how seductive she was; how her cold body laid up against mine with her leg draped across me. I remembered her laying on top of me. I remembered the blood that dripped from her mouth and her shoulder. Later, I remembered being trapped and how she disappeared right after I yelled.

"You were—never mind."

"Toby, the next thing I remember was when you thought I possessed Alex's body. It wasn't me. Daryl had a hold of me, too; he had both of us. That's why I didn't move out of your way when you walked past me to go to your office. He had total control of me. I knew what was happening but couldn't do anything about it. All I remember is you reaching out your hand. When your fingers joined with Alex's, I could feel it too. I want to feel you again, Toby. I want to feel what real love is."

"I'm not willing to have secrets." I said defiantly.

"Alex has secrets—"

"I don't care," I interrupted. "I don't care that she has them, and I certainly don't care what they are."

"Yes, you do."

"I don't."

There was a chill on the left side of my face. I had gotten used to the sensation and it somehow put me at peace. I closed my eyes when I felt the same sensation on the edge of my lips. She whispered, "You would if you knew."

My shoulders relaxed. I licked my lips lightly and exhaled slowly. "Sara," I whispered back.

I shook off the trance-like feeling and stood up, "I have to get ready to go tomorrow."

"Take me with you."

"But I thought you said you couldn't even go outside."

"I can't," she said sweetly. "But it doesn't mean I can't be there in your mind."

"I'm done with you, Sara. I've told you, I'm with Alex. I choose to be with Alex and I won't let you get between us again."

I didn't hear from her again that night, which I was okay with because it gave me the chance to finish getting ready for the next morning and go to bed.

My alarm sounded at 5:00. I prepared coffee from the single-serve brewer before getting in the shower. I got myself ready, put ice in the cooler, loaded the Sorento and was on the road by 6:00 after locking up the house.

My thoughts during the road trip spanned from house improvements to preparations for my friends' visit the following week to Anna, Alex, Sara and all the events of the previous two months I had lived in the house. I arrived at Sam's office a little after 1:00, so I continued past and drove to a restaurant since I hadn't eaten all day. Being in the city again was like being strapped into a bumper car on a roller coaster of emotions, without a safety bar that only rode backwards. The forty-five minutes I spent at the restaurant taunted me as thirty years of memories danced around, teasing me as if to sing, "you can't have it."

I paid for my meal and got to Sam's office a few minutes early. He greeted me with a friendly man hug.

"It's so good to see you," he said.

"Thanks."

"You okay?"

"Is it obvious that I'm not? It's just really hard to be back in Indianapolis."

"Well, then, let's get this out of the way quickly." He pointed me to an office and I accepted his offer for a bottle of water. He came back with a copy paper box and sat it on the floor behind me.

"What's that?" I inquired.

"It's, uh—it's your mail since you left. You must have forgotten to submit a forwarding address."

I could only imagine what was in that box. Old bills, disconnect notices, junk mail and inevitably, I would have to sort through innumerable amounts of items addressed to Anna.

Sam continued, "I took the liberty to separate some of it. I hope it helps. Anything addressed to Anna is in a separate, smaller box. I also put a ribbon around the letters addressed to her or 'current resident.' I figure that's obvious junk mail."

"Thank you, Sam. I really appreciate it," I said as I stared at the box.

"Hey, congratulations on the house. I hope you're happy with it. I did the best I could for you."

"Damn, Sam, you did everything for me. I'm grateful for everything you did."

"Ah, here they are," he said as he greeted the buyers. They were a young couple who appeared to be in their late twenties, with a toddler. They had to sign far more documents than I did. Being the pal he's been for close to thirty years, Sam had me sign everything first and passed the documents we both had to sign over to them. The first form he put in front of me was a 'change of address' card which he took back as soon I signed it and whispered, "I'll take care of this."

When I signed the last closing document, he excused himself from the table and walked me out of the building. I put the box of mail on the ground just outside the doors and hugged him, "Thanks, Sam. This means so much."

"Take care of yourself, buddy."

"I will."

"I'll get the change of address dropped off today."

"Thanks, man."

The whole meeting took less than thirty minutes for me, so I filled up my gas tank and got back in the interstate to go home. When I got

South of Shelbyville, I called my old boss. I guess, technically, he was still my boss, but he wouldn't be after that call. I pushed the voice activation button and said, "Call Paul."

"This is Paul, how can I help you?"

"Paul, it's Toby Miller."

"Holy shit, man. How are you?"

"As good as I can be. Not bad, I guess."

"You ready to come back to work?"

"Well, that's what I was calling about. I'm in a financial situation where I can semi-retire."

"Oh, that's great—for you, I mean. Not for me, but I'm happy for you."

"Oh, shit, Paul! I still have personal things in my office, don't I? I didn't even think about it."

"I figured this was coming, Toby. I gathered all of your personal things and have them in some boxes here for you, ready for you to come back and redecorate if you wanted."

"Any chance I can have you send them to my new place? I just closed on my house and being back in Indy kind of sucked on my emotions. I'm not sure I can do it again. I'll pay for it."

"We're a multi-billion-dollar company, Toby. I don't think shipping a few boxes will take us out."

I laughed and said, "I sure wouldn't think so."

"I've hated losing you, man. It's not the same without you."

"Thanks for that, but we both know, once you announce I'm gone, people will forget me, and that's the way it should be. Everybody will move on after a few weeks."

"Some are harder to lose than others, Toby. You're right, we'll move on, but it won't be easy. It hasn't been for the last two months. I wish I could capture everything you have in your brain."

I laughed hard, considering the events in my life since I had talked to him last. "You probably wouldn't want that now, man."

"But your ideas; you were always thinking out of the box."

I hated corporate cliché phrases, particularly that one.

"I never found that damn box, Paul."

"I know; that's what made you so good. Thanks for everything you did for us through the years—and for me. You made my job easier to come in to every day."

"Thanks, Paul."

"You take care of yourself, Toby Miller."

"I will, man. Give everyone my best."

"Sure thing. See ya."

"Later."

I ended the call from the steering wheel and reached in the cooler on the floor of the passenger side to get out a bottle of water. I pushed the power button on the radio and it played my 'Driving Music' playlist. I cranked it up when the first song that came on was a classic from Judas Priest. I weaved in and out of traffic, drumming on the steering wheel, breaking the law myself. When I looked down and noticed I was going ninety-two miles an hour, I let off the gas, looked into all my mirrors, turned the radio down and merged into the flow of traffic when I saw no flashing lights behind me.

"Damn, I love this truck," I said out loud, then thought of Rick, the owner of the bar I had to get Alex from and his deep Southern accent, "*You know that's not a truck, right?*"

"Sorry, Rick. I love this SUV. Woo Wee!"

The hours of driving and the sun and shade alternating on the windshield as the sun dropped behind the Kentucky hills tired my eyes. I sat up straighter and stretched my legs with the cruise control engaged, stretched my head from side to side then reached into the cooler to get a soft drink for the caffeine.

I stopped in Corbin, as usual, filled up the tank and got a large coffee to help stay awake for the rest of the drive. I then walked around a little to stretch my legs before getting back on the interstate.

The sun was still barely above the horizon, but the glare of headlights littered the curvy highway between the mountains.

Alex has secrets. I don't care. I don't care that she has them, and I certainly don't care what they are. You would if you knew. I want to feel you again, Toby.

I tried to shake off the thoughts, but I couldn't.

I want to feel what real love is.

"Dammit, Sara," I said aloud, trying to figure out what she wanted from me. Suddenly, I heard Alex's voice in my head.

You covered for me when I needed it and always kept my secrets—Everybody has secrets, Toby. It's not always because people don't want to share.

"What the fuck are they trying to tell me?" *Shit, I never called Alex.*

"Call Alex."

She answered on the first ring. "There you are. I was getting worried. Are you going to stay there tonight?"

"No, I'm on my way home. I just crossed over the Tennessee line. Sorry I didn't call before."

"You okay to drive the rest of the way?"

"Yeah, I'm fine. I got a large coffee in Corbin and I'm full of caffeine. Come to think of it, I'll probably need every rest area from here to home. How was your day?"

"It was good. Got a lot done. I forgot to get the family videos from you."

"There's plenty of time. No reason to rush."

There was silence for several seconds. I looked at the dashboard display screen to see if the call was still active.

"Alex?"

"Yeah."

"I thought I lost you for a minute there. I'm in and out of valleys, so my reception is sketchy."

"That's okay. Will you send me a text or call when you make it home?"

"Of course, I will."

"Everything go well at closing?"

"Yeah, mostly. I have a box of mail I need to go through though. I didn't submit a forwarding address to the Post Office when I moved."

"You let me know if you want help with it. I'm sure that won't be easy. It wasn't after Sara died."

"Thanks, Alex."

"You take care now and let me know when you get home, okay?"

"I sure will." *I love you.*

I was about to say it when the phone disconnected. I exhaled hard, "Just say it, ya prick." With a deep breath, I stretched my arms out in front of me, steering with my forearms for a few seconds.

It was dark when I got East of Knoxville. I had stopped at two rest areas already, which also helped to keep me awake to make it the rest of the way home. Being Friday night, in the summer, there were a lot of other vehicles on the road that night.

I was between exits when I saw her at least a quarter-mile ahead. What was she doing there? I alternated my focus between the traffic in front of me and the little girl in the white dress and long, dark hair standing with her arms at her sides. She was looking straight out at the interstate, focused on—nothing.

Why the hell can I see them?

I got home after 10:00 and sent a message to Alex, as she requested, once I got settled.

FRIDAY, JUNE 29 10:24 PM

I'm home.

Good. Thanks for letting me know.

YW. I'm so tired. I'm going to crash out.

Ok. Goodnight.

Goodnight.

Chapter 6

Where's My Sister?

I woke up late on Saturday morning and my mind raced.

My friends are coming in on Monday and I have nothing prepared. What food do I have? What food should I buy? Are there enough places for everybody to sit? I probably need to get beer and liquor. What's the weather supposed to be like while they're here? Mail. Dammit, that box from Sam is still in the truck. That's going to suck. I need to mow the lawn.

I sat upright in my bed and yelled so she could hear me from anywhere in the house, "Sara?"

I waited for a minute before I called out again, "Sara."

"Yes?"

"Will you clean this place up and go shopping for me?"

I laughed hard and fell back down onto the bed.

"I would, honey, but I'm afraid I have a slight case of death. Maybe I'm just dehydrated, but you better do the shopping yourself this time."

I laughed harder before she even finished. "Well, what good are you, then?"

She appeared at the foot of my bed, "Give me the chance and I'll show you."

"I bet you will."

I stood up and walked to my dresser to get my pajama pants on. I brewed a pot of coffee and called out again, "You know I have friends coming to visit, right?"

"Yes."

"Will you, uh—I guess try not to—"

"You don't want them to know I'm here."

"Not everybody is comfortable in a haunted house," I said.

"Toby, I don't like it when you say that."

"What would you prefer?"

"I don't know, but I don't like it when you say I'm haunting this house."

"Well, it's the truth, Sara. Okay, not everybody is comfortable of your presence here."

"Perhaps they will be."

"Please?" I pleaded.

After a brief hesitation, she agreed, "I'll try."

"Thank you."

I got my phone to call Alex from the bedroom.

"Well, good morning, sleepyhead," she answered.

"Good Morning. I might need your help."

"What do you need?"

"I've never hosted visitors like this and I'm not sure if I'm thinking of everything."

"You're a man, so you're definitely not thinking of everything."

"You already took your sassy pills this morning, I see."

"I don't need pills for it. It's natural."

"Seriously though, I just need help making a list of things."

"What are you going to feed them?"

"I really don't know. I'm sure on Wednesday we'll do a basic cookout. I can do steaks some night."

"Do you have paper plates and plastic ware so you're not spending all of your time in the kitchen? What about drinks?"

"I already thought of beer and liquor for them."

"You going to serve them vodka with breakfast? What about soft drinks, water and juice? Seriously, Toby? You didn't think of that? Oh my, why don't I just shop for you."

I put my fists above my head like a boxer celebrating a win, and spun around, then said, "Oh, you don't have to do that."

We talked for twenty minutes as she drilled me with questions about food, drinks, entertainment, decorations, laundry and one thing that would have caused a major problem. Sure, I had a three-bedroom house, but one of them was an office and there were only two beds in the house.

While Alex shopped for groceries, I hitched the trailer to the back of the truck and ventured out to get a new bed. As far as entertainment, one night, we would spend at the gazebo. My plan was to buy the bed, bring it back, set it up and go back out to rent two four-wheelers for a week. The furniture store was offering free delivery as early as Monday morning, so I scheduled the delivery and drove into Gatlinburg for the four-wheelers.

I spent the next couple of days cleaning the house and tidying the landscape. Monday morning came and they delivered the bed right on schedule. I went to the store to get linens and a comforter.

MONDAY, JULY 2 11:08 AM

Hey, buddy. We're on our way. GPS says we should be there around 6:00.

Awesome. I can't wait to see you guys.

Us too.

I looked around the house and realized there was nothing more I could do to improve it. I couldn't clean another surface or dust anything else. After dusting, vacuuming and cleaning so much the previous few days, dirt didn't have a chance of even settling on a surface. I looked through the cabinets and the freezer to see what Alex had bought. Between the options of burgers and hot dogs or a nice steak, I figured I'd keep it simple since they were traveling all day. I scheduled steaks for Wednesday night at the gazebo.

I looked at the weather forecast in the morning and the next few days would be unseasonably cool, getting down to the middle sixties at night and only reaching low eighties through the days. To me, that was perfect and would make for excellent backyard fire weather. Before I considered myself completely ready for company, I took the time to prepare the fire pit for a nice evening fire.

I kept looking out the front window, like I did when I was expecting Alex the first time. I got the lemonade out of the refrigerator and poured it in a tall glass with ice (not to mention a bit of vodka) and sat in one of the rocking chairs to watch for them. My timing was nearly perfect. Only a few minutes after I sat down, the two vehicles turned in from behind the trees near the road. Arms were waving, wildly, out the windows.

Ryan and Shanna pulled in first, followed by Jake and Melissa. When Ryan stopped the car at the side of the steps, Shanna was looking around the car for something. Knowing her, it was a phone charger she used the entire trip that was still connected to the car. Ryan was shaking his head and laughing

"I seriously have no idea where it is." Shanna said frantically.

Ryan said, "Honey, you *just* had it. How could you lose it that quickly?"

Jake got out of his pickup truck, met Melissa on the passenger side and they walked up together, smiling when Shanna said, "Forget it, I'll find it later," and they got out of their car.

Melissa reached me first. She was looking at the ground the whole time until she got up the steps and looked at me, crying and inconsolable.

"Toby, I miss her so much," she said through sobs. I held her tightly.

"I know, Melissa, I know. I do, too."

Shanna smiled and laughed, only to lighten the mood and said, "She better not be crying, 'cause I'm going to lose it."

When Melissa let go, she stepped to the side.

"Jake! How you doing, pal?"

"Better question is, how are *you*?" he said when he put his arms around me in a manly hug.

"I'm okay," I said. "It's a hell of an adjustment, but I'm getting through it."

When Shanna reached the top step, she walked towards me and repeated, "I'm not going to cry, I'm not going to cry, I'm not going to cry."

I grabbed her by the shoulders and made her look at my face, "Then don't cry," I said with a smile as I hugged her.

"Ryan, my man. How's it going, buddy?"

"I'm doing okay, for the most part."

"For the most part? Do we need to chat?"

"Nope, not at all. Just point me to the bathroom," he laughed. "Hey, is your lady friend here?"

"No, she'll be here later, why?"

"I thought I saw somebody standing in the window, there." He pointed to the window of the kitchen that's positioned above the sink.

I fumbled over a response until I landed on, "No ladies in this house. Not even when Alex is here," I joked.

I stepped towards the door and announced to everyone, "Come on in, guys," as I opened the door. "I won't offer the standard warning that the place is a mess because I've worked on it for days. If you think it's a mess, don't say a damn thing about it." We all laughed as I held the screen door open for them.

I stepped through the kitchen and into the edge where the dining room meets the living room. "Ryan, the bathroom is the middle door on that wall," I said, pointing across the room. "I'll give a grand tour when you're done."

Melissa was still sniffling as she looked around the house. I got a box of tissues out of the bathroom and handed her a few.

She thanked me and wiped her eyes, then her nose. As others comforted her, I glanced around the house but needed a little more time than that moment.

"On second thought, make yourselves at home. You don't need me to tell you what's a kitchen and what's a bathroom."

They dispersed into different directions, which gave me a chance to look around for Sara. I had the French doors open to the master bedroom and was proud as they made comments about the stained-glass decoration above the bed.

I heard the door slide open from the Master bedroom onto the screened patio, then heard Shanna scream.

Sara, what the hell are you doing? I thought as I raced to see what was going on. When I reached the sliding door, Shanna said in awe, "Are you kidding me right now—Wow! This hot tub is amazing."

Her scream drew everyone's attention, and they all followed through my room when Ryan came out of the bathroom.

"What did I miss?"

I walked out to meet him and said, "Shanna found the hot tub."

I heard Jake say, "Dude, this really is a nice place."

Ryan followed me through the sliding glass door from the living room onto the covered patio. Melissa opened the screen door from the hot tub room out towards us. Jake and Shanna followed. Ryan walked into the hot tub area as everyone else found a rocking chair to sit in.

Shanna said, "Wow, Anna would have loved this," and Melissa agreed by nodding her head and wiping her nose again with the tissue. When Ryan joined us from the hot tub area, we all looked out at the property and listened to the sounds of nature.

"Who's this Alex chick?" Ryan asked.

Everyone else chimed in with, "Yeah. Tell us about Alex," and "How did you meet her?"

"Alex sold me this house. She's one of the best realtors in this area. She showed me around the place."

Ryan nudged Jake's arm and said, "I bet she did."

"Alex lost her sister about a year ago. I guess our pain brought us together. We sort of help each other out as we can."

Ryan asked, "And that's it? If she's just your realtor, why did you have to ask her about plans for the fourth?"

"Dude, relax man. I was only explaining how we met."

Jake mocked, "Yeah, shut up, Ryan," and they both laughed.

The laughter stopped and everyone was looking at me to hear more of how Alex and I became—Alex and I, I guess.

"Look, guys, we're taking it slow. There is an attraction there and we've been out a few times. We still talk about Anna, too."

"Is she hot?" Ryan asked as he and Jake laughed again. The ladies looked disgusted and Shanna said to Ryan, "You *would* ask that."

I tried to stall by looking around, but I knew I had a big grin on my face. "Yeah, she's hot."

Jake and Ryan gave each other high-fives and shouted, "Woo Hoo!"

Ryan looked at me again and asked with a smirk, "So, did you do it?"

"RYAN! Stop it," Shanna said.

I thought about our first kiss in the gazebo and I thought about the morning after I picked her up from Rick's. I couldn't help but smile.

"Woo Hoo!"

Jake and Ryan were giving each other high-fives again.

"She'll be here later this evening. You'll get to meet her and see for yourself."

Melissa said, "And you two boys better behave yourselves." She turned and asked, "Are you okay, really?"

"Look, Melissa, it's not easy by any stretch of the imagination, but I also don't sit around feeling depressed all the time. I'm as good as I can be, I think."

"That's all that matters then," she said with a smile and hugged me.

I asked everyone, "You all hungry?"

The common answer was that they'd rather have a few drinks first and everyone brought their stuff in. Ryan yelled from the sliding glass door, "Dude, there's a fucking bear in your backyard." Everyone ran to look.

"They come through every morning and every night. They won't bother you."

"But it's a BEAR."

"You're brilliant, Ryan. Nice identification skills, Nature Boy."

Jake laughed and the ladies stood by the glass door and watched them with, "Awe, they're so cute. Look at the little ones behind her." Shanna laughed and said, "That *one* is bouncing around on the others and running out of line."

I called out, "Keep watching the Momma. She'll turn around in a minute and get him back in line."

They gasped and Melissa said, "She just stood up. Oh my God, she's big."

"Oh, there he goes, right back in line."

A few seconds later, Melissa whined, "Come back, Momma Bear."

When we were back inside, each couple claimed the room they wanted to stay in. Jake and Melissa chose the one to the left and Ryan and Shanna were in what used to be my office. I took my desk and computer down to the basement just the day before so it wouldn't be in their way.

I lit the grill on the back patio and offered everyone a drink. Shanna got excited and said, "Oh, I found this new drink. You'll love it. Want me to make one for you?"

I knew from experience that, with Shanna's drinks, if I didn't pay attention to how much I was drinking, it would be a short night. Shanna made her drinks really sweet and *really* strong.

Everyone turned her down for the same reason I did, but within minutes, all of us were sitting in rocking chairs on my back patio watching the sun sink lower in the Tennessee sky.

Melissa got Ryan's attention and said, "What did you see earlier that made you think Alex was here?"

"When we all walked up to the porch, it looked like there was a woman standing in the kitchen."

I listened to their conversation but never turned around from the grill. In the middle of the laughter, Jake said, "Oh, that's perfect for you, Toby. Have you been on any investigations lately?"

Wow! How to answer that one—nope, no need to. Yes, Ryan, my house IS haunted and no, Jake, I haven't been on any investigations because I'm surrounded by the damn things.

"Uh, no I haven't."

"I bet there's all kind of places down here that you can go find ghosts," he said.

"Yeah, probably," I said, then changed the subject and asked, "Who's hungry?"

I excused myself from the conversation and went inside. Shanna and Melissa followed me in, offering to help. I got the meat out of the refrigerator and told them, "Alex did all the shopping for me so I have no clue what she bought to go with this stuff."

Shanna looked in the refrigerator and Melissa said, "Really? She shopped for you? Exactly how serious are you with this girl?"

"We're cautiously serious; I'll put it that way. Look, I know it seems fast and I know what it looks like. Maybe it *is* a recovery relationship. It's too soon to tell. Maybe it's not though. It's weird. When we learned of each other's loss, we connected, you know? They say misery loves company, but it's not like that with us; we don't keep each other down. We try to support each other."

"She sounds great. I can't wait to meet her."

I took the plate of meat out to the grill as the ladies prepared sides in the house. We ate outside and threw our paper plates in the fire pit. After cleaning up, I lit the fire, then Ryan and Jake helped me place the rocking chairs around it. We refreshed our beverages and watched as the fire grew and the sun crawled behind the distant mountains. We were laughing and sharing stories when Ryan looked up towards the house and said, just loud enough for us to hear, "Don't tell me that's your girlfriend; holy shit."

I turned around as Alex slid the back door closed and walked towards us wearing light-colored jeans and a white shirt off her shoulders. Her brunette hair bounced as she walked. I stood up and met her with a hug and a kiss.

"I'm nervous," she whispered.

"Don't be. I'm right here."

She sure didn't seem nervous when she spoke. "Hi, y'all, I'm Alex."

"I'm Ryan."

"Ryan, wipe the drool off your chin," Shanna said as she stood up. "I'm Shanna, it's so good to meet you."

Alex reached her hand out and Shanna said, "We're not that formal," and hugged her.

"I'm Jake," he stood up and did the same. "This is my wife, Melissa."

I gestured to the open rocking chair beside me for her to sit down. "You didn't get a drink?"

"No, I didn't think about it."

"Alex, you *have* to try this," Shanna said. The others discouraged her by saying, "No, don't do it," as they laughed.

"What is it?"

"Just try it," she said and handed Alex her glass.

Alex sipped it, looked around smacking her lips together to get the full flavor and sipped it again. "Damn, that's good."

"I'll make you one," Shanna offered and walked inside the house.

"I really like your accent." Melissa said.

"Accent?" she said. "Y'all are the ones that sound funny to me."

Most of us made small talk and Shanna made drinks. As it got later, it became as difficult to walk in a straight line as it was to control our laughter.

The fire crackled, the crickets chirped and the cicadas sang. We heard a distant coyote, then another and another until an entire pack was crying somewhere, deep in the woods.

"You," Ryan said as he pointed to Alex. "You were in the kitchen when we showed up."

I tried hard not to be obvious, but my eyes darted back and forth between Alex and Ryan. I'm not sure what worried me more; Ryan pointing it out or how Alex might respond.

"I was not. I was finishing up an appointment, drove home and just got here."

She played it so cool, I wasn't sure if she realized the possibility of Sara showing herself.

"No—you were there. It was you. I know it was," Ryan said while laughing.

Alex took her phone out of her pocket, glanced at it, then put it away before she came over and sat on my lap with her arms around my neck. She whispered while smiling, "Did she show up?"

"It appears that way," I whispered back.

We both stared into the fire. Alex rested her head on my shoulder. Her body relaxed and she nestled her head deeper into my neck. I had my arm around her and my hand on her leg, rubbing it with my thumb. She mumbled something in my ear but I couldn't understand what she said.

"What? I didn't hear you," I asked.

"Where's my sister?"

I looked around to see if anyone else heard her, but no one was looking over at us.

She continued, "I've been looking all over for her but I can't find her."

I looked around at each glowing face around the fire. Everyone was settling down and relaxing, most sliding towards the edge of their chairs. Alex sighed, "I can't find her anywhere. It's like she's a ghost."

"Honey," I whispered into her ear. "Sara's inside, like she always is."

She quietly giggled before her entire body relaxed.

Chapter 7

Gifted

“She looks how I feel,” Jake said in a raspy, tired voice.

Melissa shifted in her chair, “Yeah, me too.”

“No,” Shanna replied. “It’s not time to go to bed yet.”

Ryan flinched and sat up as though he had nodded off. “I think I was half asleep there.”

“I’d say you were all the way asleep, man.” I said as I tapped Alex’s leg and moved a little to wake her up.

Ryan yawned and stretched as he stood up. “Come on, my dear, Shanna. Let’s go.” He turned to the rest of us and said, “Stick a fork in me, I’m done.”

Alex rubbed her eyes and stirred before standing up. “It was really good to meet y’all.”

They agreed, and I grabbed a long stick to spread out the glowing embers of the faded fire before going inside.

“Always a Boy Scout, huh?” Jake said.

“Once an Eagle Scout, always an Eagle Scout, my friend.”

We all returned to the house like zombies learning how to walk again as we swayed towards the back door.

The next morning, when I woke up, I listened but heard no movement in the house. I got up, put my pajamas on and made a pot of coffee. When I opened the blinds, it seemed much brighter than normal. I turned to look at the clock on the stove. It was 10:30 and I hadn’t slept that late since I was a teenager. I heard my guests stirring in their rooms, so I made another pot of coffee. I heard pill bottles from every room in the house at different times.

Ryan walked out of their room first. I greeted him with, “Hey, buddy, how did you sleep?”

“I slept okay. The bed is really comfortable but I hope I’m not coming down with something.”

“You okay?” I asked.

“Yeah, I think so—I kept getting cold chills all night.”

Before I reacted, he asked, “What’s the plan for the day?”

My mind was still trying to process the cold chills he got all night.

“Earth to Toby,” he said.

Others were coming out into the living room.

“Sorry, man. Tonight’s the midnight parade. It gets crowded. There are probably lawn chairs along the streets already. I figured we can go into Gatlinburg and split up. You guys can take in the touristy shit and we don't have to worry about the six of us trying to agree on the same things."

By the time I finished, everyone but Alex was in the living room. Both couples agreed to the plan and Melissa suggested that if we decide that we want to do something together, we can text each other and come up with a time to meet. I gave them suggestions for attractions and went to take a shower. Alex was still lying in bed. I made her a cup of coffee and put two aspirin beside it on the nightstand next to her.

She was coming into the bathroom when I turned the water off.

"How you feeling?" I asked.

"Ugh," was all she said at first, then said, "Thank you for the coffee and aspirin."

"You're welcome."

"What's the plan for today?"

I told her what I explained to the others while she was in the shower. I brushed my teeth, got dressed in the bedroom and Alex called out from the bathroom, "What are *we* doing in town today?

"I hadn't come up with anything. Why, do you have something in mind?"

"Maybe," I heard from the doorway. She had a single white towel wrapped around her with another towel frantically drying her hair and her head tilted to the side. I exhaled strongly without realizing it.

"What's the matter?" she asked.

"Nothing, why?"

"Now, Mr. Miller, we've had this conversation before," she said as she stopped rubbing her hair and leaned on the doorway.

I took a deep breath and smiled at her. "You're just so beauti—what did you say?"

She laughed at me and said, "What's the matter? Can't pay attention?"

"Well, not when you're—when you have—forget it." I laughed at myself and repeated, "What did you say?"

"I said, Mister Shallow—"

"Shallow?" I teased.

She didn't elaborate; only repeated, "Have you ever been to a psychic?"

"Once." I said. "Anna and I had a reading during our honeymoon."

"Really? What was it like?"

"It was pretty normal at the time. Nothing crazy or super weird. What makes it strange is recalling the conversation years after the fact."

"In what way?"

"When we went, it was several days after our wedding. As we sat there, the reader asked, 'Which one of you is the photographer?' Anna and I looked at each other and I explained to her I had been taking a lot of pictures the previous few days, but I was no photographer. She replied with, 'Keep doing that,' like it was obvious. It was weird because we got married in June and the things furthest from our minds were photography and the visit to the psychic after we got back. Right until she bought me a new digital camera that year for Christmas. Several months later, I was looking at some pictures on the computer I was proud of and it hit me. I walked downstairs to Anna and asked if she remembered going to the psychic and reminded her she had asked who the photographer was."

"Oh, that's wild," Alex said.

"Yes, it was, but I haven't been to one since then, why?"

She rubbed her hair between two parts of the towel again and said, "I've never been to one. Will you go with me?"

"Sure, I'd go again. When?"

"This afternoon." She said, excitedly.

"Okay, why not!"

We all left mid-afternoon, found a parking area in the middle of town and agreed to meet back at the cars at 10:00 if we didn't see each other before that time.

We walked along the side street and each couple separated when we reached the Parkway. Alex asked where the psychic was that Anna and I saw.

"It's on the far North end of town, past 321."

"Do you know if it's still there?"

"I've seen it. It might not be the same psychic, but the place is still there."

We held hands through the thick crowds of people bustling around the streets. There were horns honking in frustration at the gridlocked traffic and people yelling, "Come on," at other drivers, while others laughed in their cars with their windows open and music blasting. As we approached the psychic, there was a young couple walking down the street with white T-shirts on. His said 'Groom', and hers said

'Bride'. They were radiant with happiness, hand-in-hand, and he leaned over to kiss her as they walked.

Walking into the building was like stepping into a different world. The door closed behind us and the sound from the streets faded. There were candles lit and ambient music played in the tiny room with two chairs on each side of a small table. There was only one door on the right wall as we walked in.

"Should we knock?" Alex whispered.

"I don't know. What if she's back there with someone now? I'd hate to interrupt."

"She knows we're here," she said.

I glanced at her with my eyebrows together. "How do you know?"

"She's psychic," she whispered back.

We tried to hold our laughter in, but failed. I couldn't look at her. Every time I did, I laughed even harder. We each looked to opposite walls, away from each other, wiping tears from our eyes and trying to regain our composure. As we did, the door opened and a young woman, who looked quite normal for a psychic, greeted us. Her appearance wasn't stereotypical.

"Hi, do you have an appointment?"

"No, ma'am," I said. "Should we have made one?"

"You're not from around here, are you?" she asked in a deep Tennessee accent.

"Not originally, ma'am. I moved here about three months ago."

"You're cute. I like your accent," she said.

I turned to Alex with a surprised look and she said, "What? You do have a cute accent, you know?"

I smiled and said in my best Tennessee accent, which wasn't very good, "Well, thank you, ma'am."

We turned back to the young lady when she answered, "No, you don't have to have an appointment. Are you wanting a reading on something specific or a general reading? The general reading includes a little of the past, your current situation, relationships, money, and family. She'll give you the opportunity to ask specific questions at the end of your session. If you want to do the general reading, it's an hour."

I decided for us and told her we wanted a general reading. I paid right away and she told us, "Now you just sit tight right here in these little chairs. Madame Rose will be with you momentarily."

She walked back through the door and Alex asked, "Is it scary?"

"No, it's not scary. It is a little weird, from what I remember. The lady we had years ago had a straight face the whole time and never really smiled. There's no crystal ball or anything crazy like that."

The door opened and Madame Rose invited us in with a wave of her hand. We stepped to the side when we entered the room and she closed the door behind us. She spoke slowly. After greeting us, she asked us our names.

Alex said, "Why don't you tell us our names?" with a slight laugh.

Madame Rose smiled and said, "It doesn't work that way, my dear."

We introduced ourselves and she walked us to a table in the middle of a larger room that was also dimly lit. As we sat down, I noticed she was looking at me without expression. Although it made me uncomfortable, I smiled at her.

"Tell me a little about yourselves," she said, but kept looking at me.

"As I said, I'm Toby Miller and just moved here from Indiana about three months ago."

"Hmm," was all she said before turning to Alex.

"I'm Alex Reagan and I've lived here all my life."

"What do each of you do for a living?" she asked.

I started. "I recently quit my corporate America job to write and photograph landscapes."

Alex jumped in, "I'm a realtor."

"You're successful." Rose said after a pause.

"I'm doing pretty well, yes."

She looked at me again and said, "I don't typically ask for this, but would you each be willing to let me hold something of yours in my hand?"

Alex and I looked at each other with approval and she reached in her purse as I reached into my pocket. I handed her my keys and Alex gave her a tube of lipstick.

"It's always interesting to know what people will hand over," she started. She held the keys up and said, "I can go anywhere I want." She held up the lipstick and said, "and I can look great doing it."

We laughed at the unexpected humor. She held our things in each of her hands. We watched intently as she sighed, moved the things around in her hands and closed her eyes occasionally.

"Hmm," she said again.

"What is it?" I asked.

She opened her eyes and placed the objects on the table, still touching them. “There’s so much sadness—hmm—that’s what brought you together.”

She looked at me and spoke, “Um, Erin, Emily, uh, perhaps an A, like Amanda or—Ann.”

“Anna,” I said.

“Yes—I’m so sorry. How are you?” she said as she reached across the table and touched the back of my hand on the table. When she did, she smiled. Her face took on an expression of pleasant surprise.

“I’m okay, I guess. Some days are harder than others, but considering it’s still new, I guess I’m as good as I can be.”

“It will keep getting better,” she said. “I will not say ‘easy’ but it will get better. You don’t like the word ‘easy’ anyway, do you?”

Any laughter we were holding onto from walking into the building had subsided.

“No, ma’am, I don’t.”

She turned to Alex, “You’re holding on to something; something heavy—hmm—something you’re not ready to talk about.”

Alex didn’t respond verbally or through body language.

Madame Rose continued, “Alex, you have to ask yourself—why—what do you hope to gain from it, hmm?”

Alex nodded her head.

Rose addressed me again, “May I speak freely, Toby?”

“Of course.”

“You’re gifted. I could tell when you walked in and again when I touched your hand.”

“I’ve had experiences, yes.”

“If you want to develop the gift, you must first accept it. It’s up to you.”

“Okay.”

“Can you tell me about some of them?”

“The first one I remember, I was a teenager, still living with my parents. My Dad was away for business. Mom and I had discussed hearing footsteps before. I always slept with my door closed. For several nights in a row, I would wake up with my door open. I asked Mom about it and she said she never opened it. After three nights of the same thing happening, I went to bed and told Mom I wanted to try something that might seem strange. I locked my door with her on the other side and asked her to confirm it was locked. She turned the handle and said, ‘Locked up tighter than a drum.’ I told her I loved her and we went to bed. I was woken up in the middle of the night by the sound of my door slamming open against the wall. I sat up in bed, staring at the wide-open door. Moments later, I could follow the footsteps getting closer to my bed. I somehow found the courage to stand up and say, ‘Look, I don’t know who you are or what you want, but you’re scaring us. You can stay here all you want, but you have to stay in the attic.’”

I looked down and shook my head, then lifted it and continued, “I’ll be damned; I heard the footsteps walk out of my room and down the hallway. A few minutes later, I heard creaking in the ceiling above me."

"You never told me that," Alex said.

"Before my Mom died, I asked her if she ever heard footsteps in the house anymore and she said she did, but they were always in the attic."

"You've had a recent experience. Tell me about it."

"We were on our way back from Cades Cove when—"

"Not that one," she said. "Something sinister—um, I see a child's toy."

I heard the notes of the jack-in-the-box play in my head and looked at Alex. We both became very uneasy; shifting in our chairs. I looked back at Rose and began, "Her sister passed away a little over a year ago. She's still in the house I live in now."

"I sense a proper name; elegant—Cecelia—hmm."

"Seraphina," Alex blurted out.

"But you call her Sara."

"Yes."

Rose addressed me again, "There's more."

I was uncomfortable again and I rubbed my hands on my shorts.

"Yes. Her ex-husband paid us a visit a few weeks ago—Daryl. He's angry. He fought me. I lost. His eyes were black and crazed. His face, scruffy."

"You saw him?" Alex said.

"Of course, I did—wait; you didn't?"

"No!"

"Tell me you've seen Sara," I said.

"Just a shadow across the floor and a glowing white figure by the back door that one time."

"But you can't *see* her?" I asked.

"No—Oh my God, you *can*?"

"Yes. I've seen her several times, like the couple at the bend last Wednesday." I reached my hand out to her, and she placed hers in mine. "I didn't ask for this, Alex. I'm sorry. I thought you saw her too."

Her lip tightened when she said, "I wish I could."

The rest of the reading was a blur. I kept hearing Madame Rose's voice in my mind, *you're gifted.* I thought of Anna but accepted that seeing her was only my imagination. I thought of Sara, then the apparition I saw that time in the Peach Orchard, and the couple I saw the week before; then I thought of the man in the back of the truck at the bend at 82nd Street and Sargent Road.

Gifted. Accept it. Do I even want this? If not, how do I get rid of it? What happens if I accept it? I've communicated with entities and have seen one running for his life; not to mention talking to the one last week. So, what if I accept it? Then what? Are they just going to come ring my doorbell? "Um, hi, is Toby here?"

I shook my head.

Gifted—sometimes, I'm not sure why it's called a gift.

As much as I questioned it, my so-called, gift intrigued me.

Chapter 8

Midnight Parade

As we were leaving, Rose handed me her business card and said, "If I can help in any way, please call me."

"Thank you," I said as I took Alex's hand and we walked out of the building to return to the bustling streets of Gatlinburg. We didn't share the celebratory emotion of the crowd.

"You hungry?" I asked.

"Yeah," she said, still looking down at the sidewalk.

I put my arm around her as we walked to find a restaurant. We decided on a steakhouse near Stoplight Ten, on the South side of town. The wait was, surprisingly, less than twenty minutes. Neither of us spoke as we waited for our table. We only listened to the country music playing throughout the restaurant in the light atmosphere.

"Miller; party of two?"

We stood up and I nodded to the hostess. "That's us," I confirmed.

We followed her to our booth and sat across from each other. Alex grabbed her phone; an indication she wasn't up for conversation. We each ordered a beer and Alex put her phone away when our waiter served us and looked around the restaurant.

"Hey," I said. She looked at me. "What's going on in your head? What are you thinking about?"

"Oh, my! Where do I start?"

"It doesn't have to make sense or be in any order. Just explain as you think."

She laughed and said, "I'm not sure *even I* could keep up with it."

I smiled at her as she took down nearly half of her beer at once. She set it down on the table with a sigh, placed her chin close to her chest and her cheeks puffed out. She looked up at me, surprised, and said, "Excuse me."

I didn't interrupt her thoughts.

"I'm thinking of so many things, Toby. Why can't I see Sara? Is it something I can learn? Can a person develop the gift? I have an appointment Friday, but don't remember what time. I think it's at 9:00. I hope like hell Daryl doesn't come back. Did I put on any underwear this morning when I got out of the shower? What about deodorant? Can you teach me to communicate with Sara like you do? What else have you seen? Who else have you seen? Jesus, I can't believe that lady at the table back there would wear something like that; it's hideous. Can you teach me photography? Let's go hiking. Would it be painful for you because you used to hike with Anna? I sure could use a pedicure. When's my hair appointment? Am I moving too fast with you? Should we slow down? Why can't I see Sara? Will I be able to someday? Is that her choice or yours? Does she 'allow' you to see her or do you just see her? The sellers had better accept our offer on the river house. What the hell do you two do when you're home alone? What do you talk about? I wish I could have met Anna—Damn. I have to pee."

"Wow, Alex, how on Earth do you keep up with all that?"

"No, really. I have to pee," she laughed.

She slid out of the booth and stood up, took two steps and immediately turned around to grab her phone off the table.

Why CAN I see Sara? What does 'gifted' mean, anyway? Do the entities somehow trust me or do I see them no matter what? How would I do if Alex and I hiked together? Maybe it would be better to hike with her and talk about some of my adventures with Anna. Maybe I should take her on a ghost investigation to see what she thinks about it. What do Sara and I talk about and do? Damn—I don't know.

"Phew, I sure feel better," Alex said. "Did any of that make sense?"

"Based on my own thought process, no, it didn't make any sense at all, but I completely understand."

"Why? What are you thinking about?" she asked.

"So many things, like you are. What keeps popping up is what Rose called 'gifted.' What does it mean? What's involved in it and if

I accept it like she says, how much more will I see, feel and hear as it develops? It's all so weird."

We silently reflected for a moment until I spoke up, "Are you expecting a call?"

"No, why?"

"You keep checking your phone. It's a bit of an obsession. Just different, that's all."

She sighed hard and said, "You're right, I'm sorry," then put the phone in her purse. "Have they come to take our order yet? I'm starving."

Our waiter appeared at our table and said, "I'm here now, and if you're starving, Miss, you've come to the right place. Can I get you started with an appetizer?"

"Yes," Alex said. "How about pretzels with beer cheese, some hot wings, a fried onion, some chicken fingers—"

"Whoa! How many are you ordering for?" I asked.

"I guess you're right. Let's just do the pretzels."

I nodded, and the waiter jotted it down.

"Are you ready to order your entrees?"

"I don't think we're ready for that yet, but we will be when you bring the pretzels out." I told him.

"Okay, I'll bring them right out as soon as they're done."

He walked away and Alex and I sat for a moment until I spoke up, "What do you say we let all of this sink in and we can talk about it tomorrow. For now, let's enjoy the meal."

"Deal."

The rest of the meal was still quiet. We made small talk about her upcoming appointment and about my friends, saying how much she enjoyed their visit.

"Wait, is Ryan the one you were with at the bar the night you met Anna?"

I laughed, "Yes, the same guy."

"So, you were single men at the same time. I bet you've got stories."

"Oh, there are plenty of stories, but I won't share any of them," I teased.

I didn't say much more about him because I knew she wasn't listening, anyway. Her mind was far too occupied. There were times she would take a bite of her food, chew as she's staring off into a distance, and continue staring for several seconds after she swallowed the food.

We walked the streets of the town after we ate our meal, entering random shops and played a round of putt-putt golf. Anna and I played putt-putt a few times too, but that day, we only went into places that Anna and I had never been. With little conversation all afternoon, I took her for some ice cream which still didn't prompt much of a response. Even when I offered ice cream, she had an aloof response of, "Sure, if you want to."

"Alex Reagan," I scolded.

We stepped out of the path of foot traffic with our ice cream cones.

I smiled when I said, "If you don't snap out of it, I'm going to put that ice cream cone right into your face."

"I'm sorry, Toby, I just—"

"You're just in a bad mood. If there's something I, or anyone else, can do to fix it, please tell me, but if there's not, well, I guess it's up to you to decide if you're going to enjoy the rest of the day or not."

I looked deep into her hazel eyes and lifted her face up to mine and pleaded, "Please."

I saw the corner of her mouth move slightly. "You can do it," I grinned. She turned away from me when she broke out in a full smile. "Whatever it is, honey, please let it go; if only for tonight. If you can't," I said as I sat down on the ground, "I'll be glad to sit right here and we can talk about it until you feel better."

She shook her head, still donning her beautiful smile, pulled my arm and said, "Get up, you silly man."

"We good?"

"We're good."

"Good. Now tell me your middle name so if I ever have to do that again, it will have far more impact than just shouting out Alex Reagan."

She laughed a little and said, "Marie."

"Alexandra Marie. That might be one of the most beautiful names that have ever crossed my lips."

"Now you're just being chivalrous," she said when she looked me in the eyes again.

"Oh no, you're not going to kiss me again, are you? Because you're a girl and girls have cooties."

"I just might, Tobias—hey, what's your middle name?"

"Ass," I said. "Toby Ass. When you say it fast, it sounds just like Tobias."

"You *are* an ass, Tobias."

"It's Lee."

"Tobias Lee Miller," she repeated.

"At your service, my dear," I turned and offered her my arm and we started walking again.

"I couldn't help but notice," I started. She looked up at me as we walked. "The way you lick that ice cream cone. It's very sensual."

Without notice of any kind, she took her ice cream cone and smashed it into the side of my mouth.

I laughed hard but froze as I licked the ice cream off the sides of my cheeks the best I could.

"You know," she started. "The way you lick that ice cream off your mouth is kind of sensual too."

I put my ice cream on her face. She squealed and I pulled her towards me and we kissed, right there in the flow of all the people.

At ten o'clock, we met my friends at the parking garage, just as we planned. Melissa and Jake were there first. He had her leaned up against his truck.

"You guys think you're teenagers again? Have to hide in the parking garage to make out?" I joked.

They disconnected and turned around in shock. I heard Shanna yelling before I could see her, "That looks like fun. Are we skipping the fireworks?"

I shouted into the air, "WHERE ARE YOU?"

"There they are," Melissa pointed across the street. Shanna broke out into a run and Jake yelled out, "Don't run. Remember when you tripped over the curb a few years ago?"

Once they got under the roof of the parking garage, Ryan shouted, "LET'S GET THIS PARTY STARTED!"

I thought of how this might look to Alex, so I turned to her and said, "We have a lot of fun when we get together. It's not too much, is it?"

"Hell no. If I hadn't drunk Shanna's drinks last night like I was a starving woman in the desert, I wouldn't have fallen asleep out there."

Shanna walked over to Alex, hugged her and slurred, "That's my girl."

"Where do we go from here?" Jake asked.

Ryan popped the trunk of his car, opened a cooler and said, "Why don't we give it a few minutes, Jake. What's the rush?"

He passed beers around to all of us and we shared stories of our afternoon adventures. Jake and Melissa's highlights were going to the aquarium. Shanna and Ryan went into shops and ate on the roof of a Mexican restaurant, then stayed there people-watching the rest of the afternoon, drinking margaritas.

As we finished our beers, we walked towards the Parkway up the side street from the parking garage. People in lawn chairs packed the sidewalks, and the road was closed. We found a space big enough for all of us to sit at the edge of the curb. Ryan nudged my arm several times and pointed out attractive women. I nudged him back once and pointed to Alex.

"Touché," he said. "Well played, my friend."

Shanna said, "What's going on?"

"Nothing, dear," Ryan responded instantly while laughing.

I leaned over to Alex and whispered loud enough so she could hear, "Nothing is always something, right?"

"Right," she replied with a grin and then leaned in to kiss me. She licked her lips and said, "You still taste like mint chocolate chip."

I heard what sounded like a coin dropping on the ground. A group of five kids screamed to go chasing after it in the street.

Jake nudged my arm and pointed to them, "Will you look at that shit."

"Tell me about it. Anna and I experienced this same thing a few years ago. Wait until one of them rolls around in a big circle."

He laughed and watched as adults threw coins in the street and the small group of kids became a toddler mob, pushing each other over when they heard the distinct, deeper sound of a quarter.

A large boom, like a cannon being fired, sounded off at midnight, signifying Independence Day and the start of the parade.

"Happy Fourth," everyone exchanged among cheers from the stretch of 1.8 miles of the populated streets of Gatlinburg.

Shanna walked over, hugged me and kissed my cheek, "Thank you."

"For what?"

"For your service."

Others joined in, shaking my hand and hugging me, "Thanks for your service, Toby."

It made me uncomfortable. I considered the changes the country had been through just in my lifetime and all the men and women that stepped up to the challenge, being away from their families, losing each other; if not physically, then mentally.

"Look, thanks guys, but I don't deserve the recognition. I was never deployed, so I didn't really do anything."

A deep, scratchy voice said from behind me, "That's bullshit." I turned around to see a man sitting in a wheelchair with only one leg and scars covering his face. His hat had the words 'ARMY VETERAN' across the front.

"Why is that bullshit, Sir?" I asked.

"You volunteered, didn't you? You served." He seemed frustrated when he said, "Tell me; what would you have done if your unit was called up?"

"I would have gone. I mean, that's an easy decision."

"Then I say—thank *you* for your service."

I smiled and said, "And I thank you, Sir."

I turned around to continue watching the parade. Alex put her hand on my arm. My friends all looked at me.

Ryan spoke up first, "You alright, dude?"

"Yeah, why?"

I looked into each set of eyes staring at me. Melissa asked, "Who were you talking to?"

"That guy, right behind us," I said as I turned around to point him out.

It was like everything disappeared around me; not only the people but all of my senses. I experienced a mix of shock and embarrassment when I noticed there was no one there. I looked over at Alex and said, "Why is this happening to me?"

I got dizzy and started swaying. Everything seemed to move in slow motion. My friends helped me sit back on the curb. I put my elbows on my knees and my head in my hands, looking down at the street as all my senses returned and I was just another stranger in the crowd of people on the edge of the road while another high school band marched by in perfect step. Alex was on one side of me and Melissa was on the other with their arms around my back.

"Come on," Alex said. "I'll take you home. Where are your keys?"

"I'll go with you," Melissa said as she turned to Jake. "Take them home tonight. We'll come back and get their car in the morning."

I gave Alex my keys. When we got to the truck, Melissa said, "You need to lie down; you're still dizzy." She opened the back door for me and followed me in when Alex got into the driver's seat. Melissa guided me to lay my head in her lap. When I did, all the visions flashed in my mind, one right after the other.

My bedroom door flew open with a crash. A man was running for his life across the Peach Orchard, I saw the man sitting in the back of the pickup truck with a dark coat on, a ball cap, jeans and work boots, saying, I'm so sorry. I saw Sara sitting at the table with a glass in front of her. You seem like a respectable guy, Toby. I'm sure your lovely Anna obeyed your every wish, didn't she?

I sat straight up with my blood pressure rising at the last thought. Melissa put her hand on my arm and said something, but no sound came out.

I saw the little girl in the white dress on the side of the road; her long hair framing her face and her arms straight down by her sides—

I saw the couple at the bend in the park, then I saw the man in the wheelchair I met twenty minutes before.

"I don't even know what's real anymore," I said aloud.

"Want to go back to Rose?" Alex asked.

"No," I replied. "not yet—fucking gifted. What kind of bullshit is that?"

Chapter 9

Toast

Melissa checked on me the entire trip back, stating, "I've never seen you like this as long as I've known you."

"You don't know the half of it, Melissa."

"Then tell me."

"If I do, you'll think I'm as crazy as I do."

"You're not crazy, Toby. What's going on in your head?"

"A million things." I looked over at her and patted her on the leg. "Thanks for being there for me."

"I haven't done anything."

"You've done more than you know, so thank you."

We stopped in front of my house, Melissa waited for me to get out of the truck and tried to help me up the steps, but I insisted that I was fine. We reached the top and Alex opened the door for us.

"Can I get you some water, Toby?" Alex asked.

"Water? Really; at a time like this?" I said as I sat on the couch.

"Coming right up," she said and brought me a lemonade with vodka.

The others weren't far behind and they started up the steps at the same time Alex brought me the drink.

Ryan and Shanna came in singing some pirate song as they stumbled through the doorway with Jake shaking his head behind them. Ryan walked over and knelt on the floor by the couch. He looked around and said, "We've known each other a long time, so don't bullshit me. Are you okay?"

"I'm alright. Let me sleep on it and I'll try to explain tomorrow."

"Ok, buddy. Let me know if I can help."

I finished my beverage and laid down on my bed in my room. I knew the others were talking about me in the living room. Although they tried to stay quiet, a drunk whisper isn't much of a whisper at all. The last time I looked at the clock, it was 1:58 AM

Being the first one up again at almost 11:00, I played coffee host like I had the day before. Sitting outside with coffee and it wasn't long before the others joined me on the back porch. Everyone was being far too obvious that they were avoiding any comments about the midnight parade. At least until Ryan asked Alex, "Hey, what were you doing in our room last night?"

I'm certain they didn't notice her fumbling to find a response, but I did. As far as they would know, she never missed a beat. As soon as Ryan asked, she took a quick sip of coffee, cleared her throat and said, "I was just checking on you. I checked in on Jake and Melissa as well to make sure everyone had what they needed."

"Oh, okay," Ryan said.

"If it made you uncomfortable, I'm sorry."

"No, it's fine. Thanks for checking on us. It just seemed a little weird that you were standing at the foot of our bed as long as you did."

She smiled without saying another word.

Jake took Ryan to get his car and we spent the day socializing, eating food from cheese, vegetable and fruit trays, then popped open a few drinks around 4:00.

"Don't ruin your dinner. We've got big plans for tonight." I said.

"What's the plan?" Shanna asked.

"We're having a cookout out at the gazebo."

"Where's the gazebo?" Jake asked.

"Oh, it's out a few acres."

No one looked excited that we had to go a few acres to have a cookout. Melissa replied with a bland, "Oh, nice," with a fabricated smile.

"Don't get so excited," I said sarcastically. "It will be fun. Come on, I'll show you."

I remained quiet while everyone refilled their drinks. When everyone was ready, I led them out to the garage, walked in the side door and pushed the button on the wall to open the bay door. The four-wheelers were lined up side by side.

"Um, Toby?" Jake said. "Why do you have three four-wheelers?"

"That's our transportation to get to the gazebo."

Smiles came across everyone's faces and they got excited. They moved fast when I asked, "Who wants to help me get stuff from the fridge?"

We packed a large cooler, which I strapped to the back of my four-wheeler that had the food and all the drinks in it. I also strapped the charcoal that Alex bought to the back and packed an mp3 player and a portable wireless speaker. We were about to leave when I remembered one other thing from the shopping list I gave to Alex.

"Hey, were you able to find new candles for the sconces when you went shopping the other day?"

She turned around back to the house and called back, "Yes, I did. I know right where they are."

We started up the four-wheelers and drove around the perimeter of the yard to the access road. I took the lead with Alex followed by Ryan and Shanna, then Jake and Melissa. We were cautious when we approached the ravine with the creek and the four-foot cascade that was fifty yards upstream. With the occasional rain we'd had, the water level was low, and the creek was only two feet wide. The cascade fell through a small break in the two large rocks and was only a few inches wide. We stopped, turned the engines off to listen and signaled the others to do the same.

"Oh my God, Toby; this is all yours?" Jake asked.

"Yes, it is."

"We'll take it slowly the rest of the way. I haven't been back here in a while so I don't know what might be across the trail. It bends back and forth a few times and there are some big trees you need to avoid. Pay close attention now. You don't want to turn off the trail once we get along the ridgeline up here."

We continued on and navigated the trail until we reached the gazebo and turned the engines off again. We walked up to the gazebo but no one spoke until Shanna whispered, "This place is amazing."

I smiled at her and we all stood still, listening to the sounds of nature all around us. The sun was beaming through the trees. I looked around at the others. It appeared everyone's shoulders dropped, which I accepted as a sign of stress relief. Melissa walked to the edge where the sun was coming in and gazed up into the light with her eyes closed. The trees swayed lightly as though dancing slowly to music we couldn't hear. There were occasional chirping birds, rustling of leaves and cicadas playing for an audience of six.

I unstrapped the cooler without speaking. Ryan and Jake came over to help. Shanna turned on some music and served drinks while Melissa and Alex sat on the swing. Conversation picked up and it wasn't long until we were all laughing and catching up with each other again. I placed the candles in the sconces on each of the eight support columns before joining the others in conversation.

"Alright," Ryan said loudly. "What the hell happened last night?"

Everyone fell silent. I looked around the gazebo at each set of eyes fixed on me, waiting for a response. I looked over to Alex and nodded, showing her it was time to share the truth; at least a version of the truth I felt they could process. Alex stood and put her arm around me, guiding me to sit on the bench seat near the gazebo entrance. I looked at her again and she nodded. Before I spoke, I put my arm around her, too.

"Do you guys remember Anna telling you about me being able to —see—things sometimes?"

Only a few responded with slight head nods. Jake paused the mp3 player.

"Alex had a sister. Her name was Sara." I glanced over to Alex one more time before continuing. "They were twins. A little over a year ago, she got into a fight with her husband. He pulled out a gun and killed her. Alex witnessed the whole thing and was the caretaker for her house until recently."

Melissa spoke up first with her hand on her mouth, "My God, Toby—this house?"

I glanced at each face again, "Yes."

After giving them time to process the information, I continued, "Shortly after I moved in, I started hearing noises. When Alex told me about what happened in the house, I was interested, so I tried to communicate with her sister, using some of my equipment."

"Did you get anything?" Shanna asked.

"Yeah—Um—" I bit the corner of my lip and sighed. "She responded to the dowsing rods and talked to me through a Spirit Box. One night, when Alex stayed in the room you guys are in," I pointed to Jake and Melissa, "she talked without equipment."

"She's still in the house, isn't she?" Ryan asked. "That's who I saw in the kitchen when we first got here."

I glanced at Alex before responding and said, "We didn't see her and I haven't talked to her in a while, but, yes, we think it was her."

"Holy fuck, so it was probably her standing at the foot of our bed last night, too."

Alex spoke up, "Ryan, Sweetie, I was never in your room last night."

Ryan looked at Alex for a moment and turned back, waiting for more.

"About six weeks ago, we had a different experience. Weird shit happened in the house for a few weeks and we thought it was Sara. What started out as weird; turned dark. Her husband showed up."

Jake jumped in, "Do we need to go kick his ass?"

"Um, that might be a problem, Jake." I glanced at Alex and lied, "Sara shot him moments before she died. He died the same night."

Alex placed her hand on mine, so I skipped forward. "Since then, I keep seeing people. We were out by Cades Cove last Wednesday and a couple drove off the road. As we got closer, I talked to them."

"Were they okay?" Melissa asked.

Alex jumped in, "I couldn't see them—only Toby could."

I continued, "I was driving across I-40 from Knoxville late Friday night."

Alex looked at me, concerned, as it was the first time she heard about it.

"I saw a little girl on the side of the interstate. She was wearing a white dress and had long, dark hair that framed her face. She never moved and stared out at the road, right next to one of those makeshift roadside memorials with the cross and wreath."

"Okay, that's fucking creepy," Ryan said.

"Tell me about it. Which brings me to last night. When I explained that I didn't deserve recognition for my service, a man was behind me in a wheelchair. He was an Army veteran, and he explained that I do deserve recognition because I volunteered. Even though I wasn't deployed, doesn't mean I shouldn't be proud of my service was the ultimate message from him."

I watched the stunned expressions and finished, "Until last night, I knew the visions I saw were—entities. The dude at the parade was so real."

Jake asked, "So, you didn't know he wasn't really there?"

"Just because you couldn't see him, doesn't mean he wasn't there. I don't know why all this is happening."

I looked at Ryan and said, "I'm sorry, man. I know you were excited about the parade."

He walked over, put his hand on my shoulder and said, "And I saw the parade. It was awesome. Thank you."

Alex spoke up, "Can we fire up the grill? I'm starving and don't want to talk about this anymore."

Everyone responded, agreeing with her in their own way. The only statement I heard amid the commotion was Ryan saying, "Glad I asked while the sun was still up, man."

"Look," I said above the others. "If you don't want to stay here tonight, I understand, but please watch how much you drink if you're going somewhere else."

Ryan immediately said, "To hell with that, I'm drinking a lot."

"Please, don't get too crazy until we get back to the house, okay? I don't want to buy these quads."

"You got it," he said.

Shanna started the music again. Everyone stirred, but conversation was scarce for several minutes until Ryan and Shanna laughed and Jake asked what he missed.

I lit the charcoal and got another beer for myself. I stood in front of the grill, looking out at the woods. Alex mingled with the others as though she had known them for twenty years.

Why is this happening to me? How do I separate the living from the dead? He was so real.

"You did good," Alex whispered, as she touched the back of my elbow. "You didn't tell me about the little girl."

"I was tired when I got back. Sorry, but I didn't think about it until I explained it. Alex, what do I do? I feel like I'm going crazy. I just won't talk to anybody I don't know."

"Try to have fun tonight—please? Mingle and have fun with your friends. Who knows when we'll see them again."

She was right. If there was anybody who could keep my mind off of things, it was my four long-time friends. As it got darker, the air stilled and I lit the candles around the gazebo as I finished the steaks. Alex got the paper plates and plastic ware out in addition to the macaroni and potato salads. As everyone finished their meals, they put their paper plates on the charcoal and the plastic ware in a shopping bag.

Chirping crickets joined the choir of cicadas and the band of distant fireworks as evening faded into night. I gathered small sticks and kindling to build up the fire in the grill and joined the others as they danced around to the music in the candlelit gazebo. As I moved around to the music and watched my friends having so much fun, I considered something else; someone else. Anna would have loved it. I stood in the middle of the gazebo, right in front of the swing and raised my beer. Shanna turned the music down and everyone gathered, also with their drinks raised up.

"The last four months have been a—"

"Disaster?" Jake said as everyone laughed.

"You could say that. The last four months haven't been easy at all. Not by a long shot. You being here makes my life seem a little—normal again. I've missed you."

"Awe, we've missed you too."

"And I miss Anna—every day."

Alex put her arm around me and kissed my cheek.

"When I stood next to Anna's bed in her, um—"

I sighed, pulled my beer down and looked up at the ceiling of the gazebo. "In her final moments—" Melissa began to cry. "She told me I needed to keep living my life. She said I needed to—live while I'm alive. As hard as that is some days; some hours; some brief moments, I'm doing the best I can."

Shanna put her arm around Alex, Ryan joined next to Shanna. When Jake and Melissa joined, we were in a full circle in front of the swing.

"She always believed in me and—her strength is my strength sometimes."

I looked over to Alex and said, "I've had someone to catch my fall occasionally, but sometimes, I need to land on my own so I can pick myself back up. I think that's what she was trying to tell me in the—in the end."

I raised my beer up in a toast again and said, "To life."

"To life," everyone responded.

My voice cracked when I finished, "To Anna."

"To Anna!"

We all came together in an embrace amid tears. Ironically, the mp3 player faded into a slow Billy Joel song, Anna's favorite. When we broke free, Melissa stepped off the steps of the gazebo, crying. I followed and gently placed my hand on her back. She turned and sobbed into my shoulder.

"Melissa, what is it? What's the matter?"

"I have nightmares, Toby."

Thinking she was referring to the stories of ghosts I shared a few hours before, I said, "I'm sorry, Melissa. I shouldn't have said all those things earlier."

"It's not that—I dream about the night she died. We were all at dinner; me, Shanna, Mary, and Anna." She chuckled. "We laughed so hard that night. The last thing I said to her was, 'See ya later.' I mean, it was so casual. I took her for granted and never told her how much she meant. In my dream, I'm face to face with her again and I finally get to tell her how I feel. She gets inches from my face and screams, 'Why didn't you tell me when I was alive?' I wake up crying every time. When we all split up that night, even Shanna gave her a hug and told her she loved her as she walked towards her car."

She composed herself, wiping away the stream of tears.

"If you ever see her—Anna, I mean," she continued. "Please tell her I love her and I miss her."

Don't come looking for me. It will only hurt both of us.

I put both of my hands on Melissa's shoulders and looked her in the eyes, "I will, Melissa. I promise. Until that happens, you need to forgive yourself. Telling someone you love them is only the words. I'm sure she knew it. The three of you were her best friends in the world—Melissa," I called her attention to look up at me. "Live while you're alive."

She nodded her head, smiled and hugged me again.

As the darkness shrouded us, we packed everything up and cleaned up the gazebo. Ryan said, "I sure hope these four-wheelers have headlights."

I was getting ready to blow out the candles but stopped. "Good point, man. Fire it up." He used the flashlight app on his cell phone to see, got it started and found the headlights. We all squinted and turned away until our eyes adjusted to the light. I blew out the candles as Jake and Alex started the other two quads.

Alex took the lead. She called back to everyone, "If you've never been off-roadin' in the woods at night, you're in for a real treat. The shadows will play tricks on you. Keep your eyes on the trail. We're going to take it slowly again."

The others nodded and followed as Alex started along the trail. It took three times longer to get back than it took to go out to the gazebo. We were on the trail so long, I wondered if she had made a wrong turn as we sunk down into the ravine and back up the other side. The trail was straighter the rest of the way, so she sped up until we got back to the garage where we parked the ATVs and unloaded all of our belongings.

"That was fun," Jake said. The others joined him in appreciation.

"What time are you two leaving in the morning?" Shanna asked.

Jake said, "We don't typically sleep late so we'll pack our stuff up in the morning and get on the road as soon as we've got it all put together."

Chapter 10

Conversations with Sara

I woke up early on Friday morning. Jake and Melissa were moving around while I was still lying in bed. Jake had already gone out to his truck at least once and came back in for more. I walked out to the living room and greeted them with, "Mornin', want coffee for the road?"

Melissa said, "No thanks, we'll be peeing every thirty minutes if we do that."

When Jake took the last bag out to his truck, he stood in the kitchen and said, "I think that's it. Thanks for everything, man. That was a lot of fun. We don't get away from the kids much, so this was needed."

"Any time at all, my man."

Melissa yawned and stepped closer.

"See ya, Toby," she said as I hugged her and kissed her on the cheek.

"Bye, Melissa. You take care of yourself."

"I will. Thank you. And thanks for the chat last night. I think it made me feel just a little better."

"Oh, good. I'm glad it helped."

I reached for the door and said, "I'll walk you guys out. You have everything?"

Jake looked around one more time and said, "Yeah, I think we got it all."

"Damn," I said. "That means you won't be turning around to come back."

We laughed as they walked down the front porch steps.

Jake turned around. "We'd love to have you come visit sometime."

"I don't know if I can do it, Jake. When I was up there last week, it was—"

"Toby," he said. "Whenever you're ready. Until you are, and as long as we're invited, I think I speak for both of us when I say we'd definitely come back again. That gazebo is badass."

"Yes, we'll come back," Melissa said without hesitating, turned and said with a smile, "Hey—I love you."

"Love you too, Melissa."

"Love you, man," Jake said.

"Love you, Jake."

I watched them from the front porch as they settled into their truck and drove towards the dirt road. Before reaching it, Jake waved his hand out the window of the truck, turned left behind the tree line and out of sight.

Back inside the house, Ryan and Shanna were milling around in their room behind the closed door to the old office. I peeked in on Alex who was still sleeping as peacefully as ever. Leaning on one of the closed French doors, I watched her with both hands around my coffee. I considered, for the first time, that she might have wanted me to wake her up to see my—I mean, *our* friends off. I strolled over to her side of the bed and stroked her arm. She smiled as she awoke and said in a raspy voice, "Coffee?"

"I'll bring you some," I grinned.

She pulled her hands up to her eyes and rubbed them with childlike determination. "Did everyone leave?" she asked.

"Jake and Melissa left a few minutes ago. It sounds like Ryan and Shanna are getting their things together now."

She opened her eyes wide, trying to force herself to wake up, sat up and said with determination, "Coffee!"

"I'll be out here," I said with a smile.

"M-kay," she said.

I filled her cup and sat it on the end of the curved, granite countertop so it was closest to her when she came out of the bedroom. When she did, Ryan came out of their room with their suitcase.

"Morning, Toby," he greeted.

"Hey, Ryan. Did you sleep better last night?"

"Yes, I did. I slept like a baby."

"Oh, no; you didn't wet the bed, did you?"

We both laughed and he replied, "No, man. I did not wet the bed."

Alex sipped her coffee and said, "You guys are fun. You need to come back again."

"That was a great time,"

Shanna came out of the room with another bag over her shoulder, "Morning, all," she said. "Ryan, have you seen my phone charger?"

"Jesus, this again? I'm gonna tie the damn thing around your neck."

Alex spoke up, "Is that it over there, in the outlet next to the couch, darlin'?"

She looked at the wall and said, "Oh, you're a lifesaver," as she walked over to unplug it.

Ryan put the suitcase in the car and came back in. He looked around one more time before giving us a hug and saying goodbye.

"Love you, dude," he said.

"Love you too, man."

Shanna came over and hugged both Alex and I before turning towards the door. We followed and stood on the porch as they got into their car and drove away. We walked back inside and as soon as we closed the door behind us, we heard her, but the words she spoke weren't as elegant as usual. "That was fun, and that Ryan—damn, just give me a body and I'll take over from there."

"SARA!" Alex scolded.

"What?"

"What the hell were you doing standing at the foot of their bed the other night?"

"Watching him. He is a pretty man."

Alex laughed and Sara said, "What, you disagree?"

"Sissy, it doesn't matter what I think. If you want to stand over people and watch them, you do what you want. Can you practice a little self-control next time though and not show yourself to avoid scaring the shit out of people?"

She spoke again in that sweet Tennessee accent, "S'pose I could have," and giggled like a little school girl.

"I was looking forward to using some of this equipment again," Alex said.

"I can go away if you want," Sara replied.

"Don't be foolish."

"Ok, Sis. What do you want to talk about?"

"You."

"I'm not interesting. Why would you want to talk about me?"

Alex looked around the living room and started several times, but kept fumbling over her words. Her indecisiveness prompted Sara to say, "Just put it out there."

Alex and I walked to the couch and sat down, interlocking our fingertips. She asked her question seriously, "Where have you been?"

"Here," Sara replied. "I'm always here."

"What made you so weak?"

"Him. There was nothing I could do. He took over in every way you can imagine."

Alex thought for a moment and said, “It’s so strange that you still get tired and weak. I thought only our bodies got weak and that nothing could hurt you.”

There was a silence before Sara spoke again. “Oh, Alex; do you remember when we were little? People called you names. They said you were fat.”

Alex glanced at me. She was angry and replied, “Yes, I remember that. I wish I didn’t, but I do.”

“It didn’t hurt, did it? You had no bruises. You didn’t get a black eye from it and didn’t need a single bandage.”

Alex held my hand tighter but never said a word. Her breathing was deeper. She bit her lip and sighed as her body tensed up.

Sara continued, “I can tell that you still feel it now; even after all these years. Why? You’re so beautiful.”

Alex took a deep breath, crossed her arms and placed her chin on her hand.

Sara spoke again, “You *know* you are and you’re still humble about it. So, I ask; why does it still hurt now? Nobody ever touched you. You hurt on the inside, Alex. And the inside; well, that’s all I have left—and it still hurts.”

Alex didn’t hold back any longer, “How are you talking to us now, huh?” Alex began. “How is it that a few weeks ago, you were here; you could talk. You even showed yourself. He showed up and you got weak. He broke you again—on the inside, like you’re saying. But here you are, weeks later; able to talk to us.”

Alex stood up and paced the living room before she continued, “Yes, I remember when I was fat. I remember how mean kids were.

You know what, Sara, I also remember the day you told me that 'fat' was my attitude, not a reflection of my weight." She sighed. "We were fourteen; not an easy time for a girl to change her attitude, but I did it. We played outside that day. It was the first time I played in weeks because of how they made me feel. What you helped me realize was that no one *made* me feel that way, but me. I gained confidence long before I lost the weight—and sure as hell didn't need a doctor to fix me. That was on the inside too, Sara. If all you have left is the inside, you're never truly broken unless you allow someone to break you—and I want my sister back."

"Alex, until a few weeks ago, I didn't think he *could* hurt me anymore, but now—well—I guess I'll have to see."

"What do you mean?"

"Right now, I'm confident that, if he ever shows up again, I won't allow him to hurt me."

Alex said, "Good for you, Sara. Really. At least, it's a start."

"But that's easy to say when he's not here."

None of us spoke. I waited for Alex's response as I listened to the fan of the air conditioner when Sara added, "I don't want to hurt anymore."

I spoke as Alex did; into the air, "Maybe he's gone for good this time."

"What, dead?" Sara said. "Like he already was? Like I am?"

"Surely, you'd know if he was here," I said. "He's nuts. He wouldn't be able to keep quiet. People like him can't help themselves from letting everyone know they're an asshole."

"Sara," Alex said as she looked around the room. "You don't deserve this. It's not your fault. So, what? You didn't see the signs sooner. Who cares?"

"I was naïve," Sara said.

"Maybe you were. Let it go."

Alex paced back and forth in the living room, looking everywhere, but had nothing to fix her eyes on. I could see the frustration increasing and she snapped, raised her voice and said, "Seraphina Nicole, you show yourself right now."

A low rumble developed across the room that vibrated the shelves all around us. Alex's hair fluttered. Her eyes were wide when she looked over at me and said, "Oh shit!" Her confidence turned to fear, just as mine did and she sat on the couch next to me again. I reached my hand out to hers; both of us holding our breath. Clouds blocked the sun and the shadows outside dissipated.

"Here we go," I said.

The rumble increased and the light breeze turned into a single gust of air that blasted through the living room.

"I'm not staying in here. To Hell with that," I said as I grabbed her hand, and we started towards the back door.

In an instant, everything stopped and her elegant voice said, "Alex."

I turned to look first, but Alex kept facing towards the sliding door. Sara sat at the dining room table in the same place she was when I spoke to her the first time. There was no glow around her. She wasn't translucent. She sat with perfect posture in the chair, blinked and asked, "Where are you going?"

Alex turned. She was void of emotion when she took a step towards the table, "Nowhere, I guess. Not now."

Sara motioned for Alex to sit at the table with her. Alex focused on Sara and followed her silent instruction when she pulled out the chair that Sara pointed to and sat down. She could see her.

"How did you do that?" Alex asked.

"Does it matter?"

I stood still, wondering who we were talking to. Her behavior changed when she let Alex know of her presence last time. I inquired, "Wait. How do we know you're not—"

Sara smiled and interrupted, "It's me, Toby. I promise." Alex and I exhaled at the same time. Sara turned her attention back to Alex and said, "Here I am. What do you want?"

"Look, Sara, you're the one who's a beautiful woman; way prettier than I am. I wish you could start over, now that Daryl's gone. To feel wanted and treated right. I wish you could learn true love. Then, you wouldn't feel as if you deserve to be punished."

Sara glanced over as Alex spoke and I looked away. Sara began again, "You know, I used to look on the internet for ways to overcome the hurt from abuse. It was invigorating; really encouraging. There were little quotes out there that changed my mind. All of them—ALL of them spoke of having the strength to leave. I learned that an abuser *chooses* abuse, and it wasn't my fault. One said, *you may have blackened my eye, but you'll never blacken my spirit*. Another said, *God, help the next girl because I promise, you'll never do that to me again*. Oh, and the classic, *what doesn't kill you...*" She laughed a sarcastic, high-pitched, "HA!" She shook her head and whispered, "Too late."

Alex sighed and Sara continued, "Look, I know I didn't deserve it. I know it wasn't my fault. There's nothing I can do about that now. I can't hurt him. I can't leave him. I can't start over."

"There *has* to be a way," Alex said.

"A way to what?"

"I don't know. I still wish the same thing for you that I always did, Sis."

"And what's that?"

Alex reached over to put her hand on top of Sara's, but it didn't stop until it reached the table and she looked into Sara's eyes.

"Peace—for you. Your version of peace; not mine or anybody else's. I wish you peace in your life; in your afterlife—yeah—peace."

Sara tried to squeeze Alex's hand when she said, "I have you. I have Toby. You bring me peace—both of you."

"That's contentment, not peace. Not the peace that matters."

"Alex," Sara said softly. "All of our lives, you've taken care of me; as I've tried to take care of you. We've pushed each other to be a little better than we were—and we did good. You can challenge me to find my inner peace, but you can't discount the peace you two bring. That's *my* version; not yours. No one gets to tell me what my inner peace is, not even you."

She faded slowly and looked down at herself, puzzled. She held her hands out in front of her face, studying her palms with an expression that blended fear and surprise. I stood from the couch.

She glanced over with her hands still up, then to Alex just before she disappeared.

Chapter 11

Protection

"Sara," Alex called out. "Sara!"

She shook her head in disappointment and said under her breath, "Dammit."

I felt differently than Alex did. It's hard to describe. Something was different that time. She had disappeared before. Hell, she did it all the time, but that wasn't her typical behavior of vanishing or to just stop talking. She looked confused; even scared. I had gotten to know Sara, as a spirit, more than Alex did, and I don't think she even noticed the strange behavior.

Alex further expressed her disappointment when she said, "Oh my God, why does she do that?"

She stood up and looked around the house. "Get the spirit box."

"Alex, she's not—"

"GET IT!" she demanded. She lowered her voice almost to a whisper, "please."

I stood from the couch and got the spirit box from the closet, took it out to the dining room and handed it to her. She switched it on with the dial and kept turning it until she maxed the volume and sauntered around the living room; pausing with each step to listen. She checked in each bedroom, then rounded the corner behind the stone wall and into the galley kitchen. Her footsteps were distinct on the tile floor with a three-second pause between each. She continued into the larger kitchen and passed through the French doors into the master bedroom.

The volume turned down until it clicked and there was a rattling thud. I knew she had thrown the transmitter into the box in the closet. As I expected, she walked out of the bedroom, but stood in the middle of the living room, put her hands on her hips and said, "She makes me *so mad* sometimes."

She walked around again and gathered her things; the last being her small purse, then came into the living room again. I stood up from the couch and asked, "Are you leaving?"

"Yeah," she said, looking at the floor.

"When will I see you again?" I asked.

She looked up at me, "I always come over here. I'll host next time. Do you have plans for tomorrow night?"

I laughed, "I never have plans, Alex."

"Okay. Come by around 6:00 and I'll make dinner for you."

"What can I bring?" I asked.

"Just you."

"Okay. 6:00. I'll be there."

"Remember how to get there?"

"Yep."

She looked around the house one more time, turned and focused on the floor again, shaking her head as she started towards the door. I followed her and watched her leave, like I always did, and walked back inside to see if I could get a response from Sara. I called for her multiple times but could only hear the hum of the air conditioner and a light clicking sound as the refrigerator finished a cooling cycle.

The day seemed to creep by. When I thought the sun should have been setting, I looked at the clock and it was a little past 11:00. I loaded the four-wheelers and returned them to the rental place in town and got a partial refund since I rented them for a week but only had them for a few days.

When I returned, I unhitched the trailer, put the truck in the garage and walked upstairs. I got a soft drink out of the refrigerator and sat in my recliner with the pleasant emptiness that goes along with the first few hours alone after guests leave. I walked around the house and closed all the blinds and sat back in the recliner to kick my feet out. As the excitement of the previous two weeks wore off, I nodded off several times. I tried to fight sleep, but it got the best of me and I laid down for an early afternoon nap. It was 1:26, and I set the alarm for 3:00 to a Shinedown song.

"Toby."

Her voice seemed to come from a distant place.

"Toby," I heard slightly louder.

Something moved on the bed and I woke up, but not entirely. I laid on my stomach with my head turned towards the sliding glass doors to the covered patio when she crawled into bed with me. The bed moved, but still, half asleep, I never opened my eyes.

"Mm," I moaned when she kissed the middle of my back between my shoulders and grazed the tips of her fingers between my shoulder and elbow. I smiled and she whispered, "Wake up, sleepy head."

"I thought you were going home." I said. The bedsheets slid down my body with her fingers still rubbing my arm past my elbow, then onto my side and down the outside of my leg. She kissed me on my shoulder and whispered again, "I *am* home, honey."

"Mm, yeah."

"As long as I'm with you, I'll always be home."

I reached my arm up to her and glided my fingers through her long, straight hair.

"I brought a friend," she whispered into my ear.

"What?"

"As I understand it, you've already met. This is Sara."

I stopped moving and opened my eyes to see the bottom of a white nightshirt. The sides curved above her hips and the front left little to the imagination as the light shone through it from the sliding door behind her. The shirt lifted when she pulled her knee up to join us on the bed. My heart raced. When she was entirely on the bed, I couldn't see her anymore; only the little girl with the long hair standing outside the sliding door, looking in with her hair framing her face and her arms down by her sides.

My mind wondered what she was doing there. I squinted my eyes in confusion.

How did she get there, anyway? I brought a friend?

I tried to call Alex's name, but no sound crossed my lips. My mouth opened and closed, but I couldn't speak. All four hands were caressing me. My body wouldn't move, no matter how much I willed it to. It paralyzed me and I was completely vulnerable. Two distinct giggles came from above me; one from Sara and one from—Jesus, is that Anna? A shaky voice sounded like it was coming from the doorway when he said, "I'm—so—sorry." A man's deep voice from the other side of the bed, near the master bathroom laughed and said, "That's what I'm talking about, soldier."

The next voice seemed to surround me from an unseen man who whispered, "Proooteeeect Herrrrr."

Then I heard them; the beginning notes of a dilapidated jack-in-the-box. His blackened eyes were an inch away from mine when he yelled, "Get out of my goddamn house."

I sat straight up and the sheets fell to my waist as I scanned the room, interlocked my fingers on top of my head and breathed fast. I looked out the window of the sliding glass door and all around the bed. There was no one in the room with me. I blinked fast and squinted my eyes to adjust to the light. I gazed up at the ceiling and exhaled strongly. I realized; at least hoped, it was nothing more than another nightmare. I stretched and got out of bed.

I put the same clothes on I was wearing before my nap and yawned several more times as I walked around the house. Something entered my mind and I didn't want to take any chances. Enough crazy shit happened the previous two months, so I walked into the spare bedroom and looked at every surface and under the bed. I was pleased to *not* see the jack-in-the-box.

I grilled hot dogs on the patio for my evening meal and went to the office to write more. As soon as I stepped into the office, I turned to walk back out, realizing that my computer was still in the basement. Not expecting any visitors that night, I mixed a drink and went downstairs. As soon as I reached the bottom of the stairs, I looked at the massive projector screen on the wall and thought of movies. I wondered if Alex ever took the Miller family videos with her, so I walked back up the steps and opened the door on the side of the right cabinet, singing the alphabet song under my breath, "H, I, J, K, L, M—there they are," I said as I ran my finger across the spine of each movie, stopping at the Miller family videos. I pulled them all out and set them on the dining room table upside down and became mesmerized by the pictures on the back covers. The scenes littered my memory like a silent movie as I stared at the small video cases.

"I can't yet," I said out loud, and returned to the basement. When I opened the document with my manuscript, I reread the last few paragraphs about the morning Amy woke me up in the hospital. Anna only had a few hours left. I continued the story and explained how the man handed me the white drawstring bag and dismissed me.

Since my nap that afternoon, I sat at my computer, writing until the only light around me was coming from the glow of the monitor. When I got tired, I looked into the corner of my computer screen. It was 2:30 AM. I had written about packing up the old house, loading it into a rental truck and moving here, to my dream home. My forever house; no, *our* forever house. Until that night, I called the manuscript *Memories of Once Upon a Time*. Before shutting down the computer, I saved the document and changed the name to *The Forever House*.

At 3:00 on Saturday afternoon, I got ready for my dinner date with plenty of time to spare. I dressed in decent shorts and a mint green polo shirt. Before walking out of the house, I sprayed a few pumps of cologne and put the Miller family videos in a plastic shopping bag. On my way, I stopped at the store to buy a bottle of Pinot Grigio for Alex and pulled up to her house at 5:54. She greeted me at the door much more casually than she did the first time; no hopping with one shoe on while trying to put an earring in. The door opened only a few seconds after ringing the bell. She was casually dressed but still looked as amazing as ever. I stepped through the doorway and pulled the bottle of wine from the bag to hand it to her.

"Oh, thank you," she said. "That's perfect for tonight."

She closed the door behind me and I looked around again. She had candles lit around the house. All the blinds were closed and there was light jazz playing from the living room to the left of the staircase. She led me to the kitchen on the right.

"Alex, I have no idea what you're cooking, but it smells amazing."

"Nothing fancy, stuffed shells, a salad, some cornbread, cheesy garlic bread, and some mixed vegetables."

I tilted my head to the side with a smile and watched her as she moved about the kitchen, stirring the contents of pots, opening and closing the oven door and stopping to finish a glass of white wine she had reached the bottom of before I arrived. When she noticed me, she pulled her drink away and said, "What's the matter, Mister Miller?"

"Nothing fancy, you say? Sure *seems* fancy."

She smiled at me and said, "Thanks."

"Here," I said as I handed her the bag with the videos in it. "Our home videos you keep forgetting. Probably better for you to watch them here, anyway."

She took them to another room, came back and said, "Thank you. I'll watch them and make sure you get them back soon."

"Take your time. There's no rush."

She pulled the lid off of one pot and an Italian aroma filled the kitchen as the steam rushed along the angle of the glass lid. She stirred the tomato-based sauce and got just a taste on the tip of the spoon, cupped her hand under it and blew on it several times before turning the tip of the spoon for me to sample.

"Damn, Alex, that's—Wow! That's really good."

"Too much garlic?" she asked.

"Not at all. It's perfect."

She opened the bottle of wine and poured a glass for me.

"I feel bad," I said.

"Why on Earth would you feel bad, Tobias?"

We eat boxed dinners when you come to my house. I took you on a date and we had delivery pizza.

She walked towards me with a smile, put her arm around me, pulled me close to her and said, "Toby, it was perfect," then kissed me. She raised her glass in front of me and I did the same.

"What are we toasting?" I asked.

"Secrets."

"Secrets?"

"Yes. All the things you've been seeing and the things we've been through together. Not many people would understand. So, I think it's best we keep it to ourselves."

"Okay. To secrets." I stated, and we sipped from our glasses.

The oven timer sounded and she turned to get hot pads to pull the shells out of the oven. She scanned them over, and when she approved of whatever it was she was looking for, poured the rest of the sauce over the shells, ground fresh parmesan cheese over the entire dish, and put it back in until the cheese was golden brown on the edges.

We ate at a tall four-top table by candlelight. The meal was so delicious, I tried to savor every bite in my mouth before taking another.

"How have you been, Toby?"

"I'm good, why?"

"Have you seen anything else? Or maybe I should ask if you've seen *anybody* else."

"No. I had a crazy dream yesterday though."

"Tell me about it."

I swallowed my food and rested my fork in my hand in thought before taking another bite.

How much should I tell her?

"It was weird. You called for me and came into my bedroom; or so I thought, anyway. You rubbed my arm and leg. You spoke, and it was—" I stopped explaining and took another bite.

"It was what, Toby?"

"It wasn't you," I said when I swallowed again. "Throughout the dream, I saw Anna, Sara and the little girl from the side of the road."

I stared at the contents of the table.

"That's weird," she said.

"Yes. The man from the parade was there too, and the guy who hit Anna and—hmm, I don't know."

"You don't know what?"

"I don't know what else or who else was there, but I know there was somebody else."

I looked over at her as she took a sip of her wine. When she put her glass on the table, I said, "I saw Daryl too. He was right in my face and yelled again to get out of his house. That's what woke me up."

"Do you have nightmares a lot?"

"No. Sometimes I think what I see in real life is worse than my nightmares. Then one like yesterday comes along."

"And you haven't seen anybody else—I mean, while you're awake?"

"No, no one at all."

"Well, that's good, I guess."

"I certainly think so," I said confidently.

We enjoyed the rest of our dinner and I helped her clean it up.

"Where's your bathroom?"

"Damn, I'm sorry, Toby. I didn't even show you around the house."

"I can find my way, if you don't mind."

"Don't mind at all. I'll clean up. There's a half bath down the little hallway off the living room on the other side of the stairs."

I looked around the living room. Everything had a place. There was a television on a stand against the inclined wall with the stairs. The wall with the front door had a small side table and a recliner and a small, two-shelf bookshelf. On the back wall stood two full-sized bookcases on each side of a window to the outside. On the other wall that ended at the hallway was a love seat with an end table. She decorated the walls with impression art and iron sconces. I walked down the small hallway which had an office at the end, a storage closet under the stairs and a small bathroom on the left. At the end of the hallway, there was an office which had a modern desk and other office furniture. I walked in and stood behind the roller chair at her clean, glass-top desk. On the right side was a stack of business cards; cards that matched the one Anna had in her wallet. I hadn't thought of the business card since I played darts a few days after moving in, but at that moment, I wondered all over again how Anna got Alex's business card.

When I finished using the bathroom, I wandered upstairs while Alex finished cleaning up. There was a full bathroom on the right with a long one-sink granite countertop, a tile shower, and a jacuzzi tub.

"This is a really nice bathroom, Alex," I shouted down the stairs.

She shouted from the kitchen, "Thanks, I sure enjoy it."

I turned around and saw a small bedroom with little in it, then continued down the hallway to the master bedroom doorway at the end. I reached the entryway to the master bedroom.

He stood in the corner of the room, by her bed. He stood straight. Although he startled me, I wasn't afraid. He was six feet tall with dark skin and wore a comforting smile and an old military uniform. My shoulders dropped and peace washed over me. A sort of calm. I nodded my head, and he disappeared.

I didn't look around the room much. Instead, I turned around and walked calmly back through the hallway, down the stairs and into the kitchen, hoping that my behavior did not differ from how it was before I toured the house.

"What's the matter?"

There goes that idea

"Nothing, why?"

"Toby."

I thought about it for a few seconds. "Alex, I—" I sighed. "I just saw a man in your room upstairs. He smiled at me. He was wearing a uniform."

She smiled. "I've sometimes sensed things here. Peaceful things though. It's hard to explain."

"That's what I was trying to explain to you last week. You just know. What have you sensed?"

"When I get stressed in my life, I come home and at some point, I get chills, then a peace washes over me and I'm not so stressed anymore; like an instant confirmation that everything will be okay. I have always wondered something though," she said as she threw her dish towel on the counter and walked into the living room.

She opened the door to one of the small end tables and pulled out a photo album. She wiped dust off the top of it and handed it to me.

"What is it?"

"It's a lawn mower; what does it look like?" she laughed.

I shook my head and sat down on the love seat with the album. She sat next to me as I flipped through the photos. There were old school pictures of a little girl with brunette hair and hazel eyes.

"This you?"

"Yeah," she whispered with a smile. "Keep going."

I scanned each image, page after page, until I came across one that made me stop. I looked at Alex, who was smiling at me.

"Who is this?"

"Why?" she asked.

"Because this is the man I saw upstairs."

Her smile broadened even wider.

"It's my grandfather on my Dad's side. I never met him. He died before I was born.

"You never met him?"

"No, but I know he's there sometimes. I've dreamt about him and he always brings me peace."

She turned the album towards herself and grinned as she looked at the picture.

Chapter 12

History

Alex rubbed her fingertips across the photograph and yawned.

"Are you tired?" I asked.

She yawned again, "Yeah, I guess I am."

"I don't want to keep you up. Should I go?"

"You don't have to,"

I leaned in to kiss her and stood up. "Thanks for the amazing meal, Alex. That was so good."

She got up and pulled a bag out of the refrigerator for me. "Here—some leftovers for you."

"Thank you, dear. At least I'll have one good meal in the next few days," I laughed.

She walked me to the door and yawned again.

"You better get some sleep. You look like you're going to pass out before I get to my truck."

When I got home, I looked at my weather app to see what the next day would be like. It was supposed to get cloudy overnight, rain in the late morning and a chance of storms in the evening. *Could be a good day for photography*, I thought to myself. *It looks like it will be cloudy again on Monday too though, but without rain, which might be better for water flow.*

My phone vibrated right after I set it down.

Alex

Saturday, July 7th 10:22 PM

I laid down to sleep right after you left. Now I'm wide awake so I watched your first two videos. They're really good.

Thanks. It was fun to make them.

I set the phone down and thought about Anna. I remembered part of one video when she was beaming because we were in the mountains. She was always at peace when we were in the mountains. I also recalled my 40th birthday on October 30th, 2012. It was cold. I was wearing a winter coat, a knit hat, and gloves. She had taken a picture of me while throwing leaves in the air, laughing. I remembered not letting the big four-oh bother me, so I acted like a kid again; even if only for that moment when Anna captured my childish behavior.

Videos, pictures—it's all too much right now.

I turned off all the lights, got a glass of milk and was in bed soon after. When I woke up on Sunday morning, I reached for my phone. There was a text from Alex.

Alex

Sunday, July 7th 2:14 AM

I completely forgot to
tell you about a
relator's conference I'm
going to this week. I'll
be back late on Friday.
Sorry, Toby.

Forgot to tell me about a conference she's going to for the week? This coming from the person who schedules every appointment in her head and never misses? Hmm, this seems odd.

Alex didn't owe me anything. I didn't need an explanation and she certainly didn't have to report everything she was doing, but it seemed strange that she forgot. Alex didn't forget anything—ever.

Sunday, July 7th 8:16 AM

Where's the conference?

I didn't get a reply. Perhaps she was driving or on a plane already. I tried to call her but was sent straight to her voicemail. Sitting on the front porch, I listened to the birds and watched the misty rain float around with the light breeze and the aroma of freshly brewed coffee rising from the cup under my nose. I placed my phone between my legs in the rocking chair in case Alex tried to contact me.

How the hell do you forget about a week-long conference? I heard Sara's voice in my head, *Alex has secrets.* I still didn't care. She kept the truth from me about the night Sara and Daryl died and when I found out, I didn't care then. Whatever it might have been; if there was a secret at all, it didn't matter and I was certain she would have a logical reason for not telling me sooner.

Where did I leave off in the book? I already wrote about saying goodbye to Ryan and Jake, I think. Oh yeah, The Forever House. I could get a lot done on a day like today.

I got up, poured another cup of coffee, went down to the basement and was able to start writing without having to reread much.

It was a productive day of writing. The memories came rushing in like a gust of wind through the trees until I got to one specific part. I had done the research only two nights before but couldn't remember the website I had found, so I pulled up the browsing history.

I was confused at what I saw. I found far more than I looked for. I found the site I was on before, but I didn't understand the rest. Why were there so many searches? Who searched?

It must have been Friday when my friends left. Alex said she had research to do and asked to use the computer.

"Oh my God," I said as I read line after line of searches. Annaliese Miller, Anna Miller, Annaliese Miller Car Accident, Anna Miller Obituary, Toby Miller, Tobias Miller, Widow Tobias Miller from Indianapolis. Annaliese Miller Manager, Annaliese Miller Family, Annaliese Miller Genealogy.

What the hell was she looking for? And why? I looked for my phone but it wasn't nearby. I remembered setting it on the counter when I got another cup of coffee. I ran up the stairs to get it and returned to the basement. When I unlocked it, there was a banner across the screen. It was a response from Alex with a single word; 'DALLAS'. She sent it twenty minutes before. How far was Dallas? I closed out of the search history and searched for the distance between Gatlinburg and Dallas. It was over thirteen hours. She had to have flown; probably from Knoxville.

Sunday, July 7th 11:25 AM

Can I call?

Again, I received no response.

"Sara?" I called as I walked up the stairs.

"Yes," I heard from behind me

"Are you down here in the basement with me?"

"Yes."

"You keep saying Alex has secrets. Do they have anything to do with Anna?"

I looked over towards the bar, hoping to see her; a question like that deserved a face-to-face discussion. I looked out the sliding glass door to the concrete patio—and over towards the theater screen. Each glance served me nothing more than the empty room I was standing in

"Sara," I said more sternly.

I walked over towards the bar, pounded my fist on the table and yelled, "SARA, tell me what's going on; please," then walked back to the computer to see what else she searched for, but there wasn't anything else. I pulled my phone out and noticed that Alex had read my last message but didn't respond, so I sent another message to her.

Sunday, July 7th 12:24 PM

I sat down to write and needed to look at my history. I saw your research. What's going on?

I looked at my phone for a while to see if she had read it, but for as long as I stared, she hadn't.

"Dammit, Sara. What are you two hiding from me?"

It didn't make sense. Alex's business card was in Anna's wallet. I confirmed that last night when I saw the same card on Alex's desk in the office at the end of the hallway. Alex has secrets. Wait!

The realization came to me. She had been trying to tell me something. When I got upset about Anna's childhood, Alex told me that everyone has secrets. She said that, sometimes, people don't keep secrets on purpose, they just don't know how to express what's in their head. *They don't know how to say it.*

Sunday, July 7th 1:06 PM

Alex, I don't care about whatever you're digging for. I do care that you're keeping it from me. Please, what's going on?

I paced the house most of the afternoon, trying to make sense of it. It was like I was trying to put a puzzle together without all the pieces. Furthermore, the box was missing, so I didn't know what it was supposed to look like when it was done.

I checked my phone several times, but the message I sent to Alex hadn't been read. *No big deal if she's on a plane,* I repeated as if I was trying to talk myself into acceptance of the strange events.

I was thankful I lived alone that afternoon because I stood in different places inside and outside the house for minutes at a time, like a statue condemned to staring in the same direction for eternity. Each time I stood, my mind flooded with sporadic events since Anna's accident on March 10. One minute, I was replaying events of that fateful Saturday night, the next, I was thinking of pulling her wallet out of the white drawstring bag. Immediately following, my thoughts flashed to the night before, seeing Alex's business cards on her desk in the office at the end of the hallway. It was an arbitrary sequence of flash memories; none leading to a sensible conclusion.

I opened a beer, walked out to the patio and tried to call again. Her phone rang twice, and I left a voicemail. "Alex, what the hell is going on? I saw the browsing history of you searching for Anna. I know I can't answer many questions, but I *have* to know what the hell is happening. Please call me as soon as possible. Text me. I don't really care how you do it, just let me know you're all right and that—we're all right. Please!"

What have I done? Was it something I said last night? Protect her. How—and from what? Protect her—protect her—shit, I wonder if she's in trouble.

I scrolled back up to her message:

> I completely forgot to
> tell you about a
> relator's conference I'm
> going to this week. I'll
> be back late on Friday.
> Sorry, Toby.

Not 'sorry, sweetie'—not 'sorry, honey', but 'sorry, Toby'. She didn't send the message. Somebody else did. She's been kidnapped. Prooooteeeect Herrrrr.

"FUCK!" I yelled out loud. The birds stopped chirping for a moment and everything fell silent. I took a deep breath, sipped my beer and calmed myself as nature's orchestra gradually returned to normal.

She couldn't have been kidnapped. That shit only happens in the movies. It's something I did; something I said. But what?

I sensed there was something behind me. It was the same feeling of being watched that I've gotten several times before. I turned and saw a ghastly, translucent image of Sara standing at the doorway, deadpan. She motioned me to come inside, and I stood from my rocking chair.

I looked around the yard before pulling the sliding glass door open. Something didn't feel right; as though I was being lured into darkness again. When I saw her hazel eyes smiling, it calmed me. I reached for the door and slid it open. Sara stepped to the side and dissipated. My anger intensified, like a thin-crusted lava dome. I closed my eyes to gain control of my emotions the best I could, took a deep breath and calmly asked, "Are you still here?"

"I'm here."

I walked in and slid the heavy glass door behind me.

"Sit," she said.

I walked over to my recliner and sat down.

"Relax," she assured.

I pulled the lever to open the footrest, which leaned the chair back.

"What is it, Sara?"

"You want something. I want something. Maybe we can help each other."

"What do you know, Sara?"

"You want to know what Alex has been up to. I'll tell you, but you have to agree to something for me."

I didn't respond. I had never negotiated in a quid pro quo scenario, and I didn't want to that day—but I *had* to know what Alex was up to.

"What is it?" I said.

"Toby, why do you ignore me?"

"What are you talking about?"

"I poured my heart out to you—and you said nothing. I've tried to touch you, but you didn't respond. Why do you ignore me?"

"Sara, this is inappropriate. I'm with Alex."

She smiled and said, "I know."

"What it is? What trap did I fall into for you to be smiling like that?"

"It's not a trap, it's something I want, but I can't do it alone."

Her cold hand touched the side of my face and she whispered, "I love you, Toby Miller."

"Where's Alex?"

"See? There you go again; ignoring me."

"Sara, where is Alex?"

There was a distant crack of thunder. I listened as it growled through the valley. I looked out the glass and saw clouds rolling in.

"Promise that you'll help me and I'll tell you Alex's secret."

"I'm not going to promise anything until I know what it is."

"Touch me like you touch her. Love me as you love her."

"Sara, I can't do that. Even if I agreed to it, I can't feel you. I told you that."

"But there's a way. I felt you before and you felt me."

"WHEN?" I snapped.

"When you came in here after Alex and I spoke privately while you were in your office."

"But you possessed her that day—or Daryl did. Fuck, I don't know. Either way, the answer is no."

"Please," she begged seductively.

"No, Sara, now where's Alex? Sara? SARA!"

Chapter 13

Face to Face

My blood pressure rose and I labored for each breath. I wanted to *make* her tell me, but still had the good sense to know there was nothing I could do to coerce her into admitting what Alex was up to. I had no leverage except the unthinkable that Sara suggested. Alex wasn't replying or calling, Sara wasn't telling me anything, so I was left to my own devices; the only problem was—I had none.

The windows shook as the storm grew closer and I lit candles all around. I had thoughts in my head I had to shake off because of a promise. The temptation grew inside me and I had never been so close to breaking a promise in my life; particularly, that one.

The room lit up and, within seconds, I heard the loud crack of thunder and the rumble of the echo. I was about to look at the weather app on my phone to see how close the storm was, and how bad it would be, but my hands shook when I picked up the phone and saw a banner across the locked screen. It was difficult to reply due to the rage that cultivated within and I tried to respond quickly. When I unlocked the phone, I saw the full message.

Alex

Sunday, July 7th 9:24 PM

Hi Toby. I made it safely. Where do I start? I'm so sorry. I'm not going to do this through a text message, but please trust me. I promise you, I'll explain everything when I get back Friday night.

Can you at least tell me why you're looking and what you're looking for? Maybe I can help you?

I watched the message show as read almost immediately but she never sent a response. "SON OF A—" I yelled while my trembling hand gripped the phone in my fist. I drew it next to my ear and prepared to launch it across the room. A vivid reminder that the person I once was, wasn't too far under the surface. I relaxed and returned the phone into its case on my belt clip.

Just this once. What will it hurt, anyway? You promised, Tobias Miller. Don't do this. But I have to know and this may be the only way to find out.

I took a deep breath

It may be the only way. I have to know. This may be the only way. I can't believe I'm going to do this.

I got the dowsing rods from the bedroom closet and returned to the middle of the living room. I sighed as I steadied the rods in my fists. I breathed deeply in through my nose and slowly out my mouth with my eyes closed. The rods steadied, and I began.

"Anna? Are you here? Honey, I need to talk to you." Tears pooled at the bottom of my eyes. I blinked, and they fell fast at first until they crawled down the sides of my cheeks.

"Anna, I—I know that I said I wouldn't—I just—I'm left with no choice. If you're here, you know what to do. Please let me know you're here."

I walked around the house several times, encouraging her and trying to contact her.

"Please, Annaliese," I pleaded. "Just this once—please talk to me." I stared at the tips of the rods. My whole body flinched when thunder struck closer than it had all night. I looked around the candlelit room as trinkets rattled together and the walls shook with the rumble through the valley.

The rod swayed in my right hand; but only slightly. I never took my eyes off the tips of the skinny brass rods when they swayed closer to each other, but never crossed.

"Anna?"

The rods flew open and bounced off my arm at the same time as Sara said, "Really, Toby? You can't even keep your promise to your dead wife? What kind of man are you?"

I held the tip of one rod in my right fist and launched it across the room. It tumbled twice before piercing the drywall next to the spare bedroom. The other slid across the wood when I tossed it on the table and stormed out to the patio. I walked to the edge, leaned on one of the support posts and watched as the distant sky lit up repeatedly. The wind blew the rain onto the patio. My clothes got heavy as they clung to my body. I stepped off the patio to the right where the deck met the ground by the detached garage. I walked out towards the center of the backyard and put my arms out to my sides, letting the rain wash over me. I tried to clear my mind of everything negative. I tilted my head back and tried to focus on the individual raindrops landing on my forehead, my eyelids, and my cheeks.

My phone vibrated. I answered it as quickly as I could, holding the phone in my left hand and covering my opposite ear so I could hear over the wind, rain, and thunder.

"Hello?" I said loudly.

"I hope you're not too tired."

I pressed the phone closer to my ear, "Anna?"

Her voice transitioned into a deep male voice when it responded, "Because I'm going to keep you up for a very—long—time."

I ended the call and ran towards the house. There was deep, wicked laughter surrounding me from all around my property until I was under the cover of the patio and it stopped. I looked out at my yard again but only saw flashes of lightning illuminate my property in such rapid succession I could see all around me.

"Prooooteeeect Herrrrr."

I put my arms out to my sides and yelled, "FROM WHAT? HUH? WHAT THE FUCK DOES SHE NEED TO BE PROTECTED FROM? SHOW YOURSELF, ASSHOLE!"

BOOM, the thunder struck at the same time as the lightning flashed. My chest expanded from the concussion and I watched a large tree limb fall from the edge of the woods, big enough to be its own mature tree. The force of the wind strengthened and I took cover inside my house.

I was dripping wet when I walked back through the sliding glass door. None of the appliances were humming nor displayed a glowing clock. There was a click as all of them flashed on briefly and turned off again. I laid down in my bed and curled up to my pillow, facing the outside wall towards the hot tub and watched the intensity of the storm which seemed like it would never end.

With each lightning flash, my imagination conceived apparitions of the spirits I had seen before. The little girl in the white dress reached her right hand out before she vanished. The Army Veteran was lying on the concrete with his face torn apart. He held his leg in his hand, looking at it in shock. The man who hit Anna stood beside Alex's grandfather. I turned onto my other side, faced away from the glass door and my phone vibrated on the nightstand.

Alex

Monday, July 8th 2:14 AM

I see there are bad storms there. Are you okay?

You don't get to lie to me, leave without an explanation, not respond to text messages, then get to ask me how I am.

I deleted what I originally typed and sent, "Yes."

A crack of thunder woke me at 5:21, but I, somehow, fell back to sleep despite my overactive mind that started as soon as I woke. Another struck close at 10:30.

I got up to make coffee and stood by the back door. The branch that had fallen the night before was even bigger than I thought, reaching the middle of the yard. My entire property was littered with several other sticks and smaller branches.

Although not as strong, it stormed off and on all day again and I was as frustrated and empty as I was on Monday. I paced the house, imagining monsters that weren't there and thinking about—everything, it seemed. Late on Tuesday afternoon, the storm passed and a light drizzle continued to fall. I gathered the tools I would need from my garage to clean up the yard and the trail.

I was in bed early Tuesday night and slept through the night, waking to a bright day on Wednesday. I checked my phone again and still had received nothing from Alex. I took my coffee out to the garage and put all the tools in the rack on the back of the four-wheeler. It took all day to clean up the debris, hauling or dragging sticks, branches, and wood to the fire pit.

As evening fell and my muscles weakened, the air was cooler. I put on a sweatshirt, put a few beers in a cooler and lit the burn pile. Mesmerized by the fire, my mind wandered. It wandered so much up to then, I didn't even know where it wandered to half the time. As the smaller sticks turned to ash, I fed the fire with piles of kindling.

The night was pleasant and was more like fall than early July. The stars were bright on the moonless night. It was the kind of night that Anna and I enjoyed so much in cooler weather. We would sit around a fire and dream of our future. A future of love, a future of photography, a future of living our lives to the fullest, a future in the forever house—a future that would never come.

The motion of the dancing fire burned into my eyes and everything seemed to move, even when I looked away from the flames. There were occasional noises in the woods that made me look up to identify the source.

As another pile of sticks burned away, I loaded the fire with more. The fire grew higher and embers popped as they levitated into the air. As I watched them, I glimpsed a figure out of my peripheral vision between the fire and the tree line at the back. I turned to look, but nothing was there.

A long, skinny branch was stretching beyond the fire pit. I pulled it out and stuck the hot end into the ground inside the fire pit to extinguish the flame from its tip and used it to push cold kindling into the middle.

What the hell?

There it was again, only closer. I looked directly and the figure was gone. I walked around the fire to get a better view, but still saw nothing. The tree line glowed from the light of the flames. Pop, crack, pop, I heard as the glowing embers lifted into the air again like fireflies racing towards the sky.

I sat back down in my chair with my elbows on my knees and the long, skinny branch resting in my hands; my head pointed directly towards the fire. I lifted my eyes and scanned the property between the fire and the line of trees.

My heart beat stronger. I gritted my teeth. I could only see him out of my peripheral vision and he disappeared every time I tried to look at him straight on. He advanced closer and became clearer. I saw his scruffy face, disheveled hair and blackened eyes.

"I killed you once, you son of a bitch, just like Alex did."

He smiled at me and never raised his voice when he said, "Calm the fuck down there, Sport, we've been down this road before and as I recall, it didn't turn out so well for you."

He stood opposite the fire from me with a sinister smile. "And," he cleared his throat. "For your information—you destroyed my host, not me. Luckily for me, I didn't make it to the jack-in-the-box before you smashed the shit out of it!"

"What do you want, Daryl?" I said as I stood up.

"Look, Tobias, let's talk—like men. I'm not here to fuck up your world like I did before." He laughed. "At least, not yet."

"Why are you here?"

"To make her life hell, like she did mine."

I heard the voice in my head, *Proooteeeect Herrrrr.* "I won't let you hurt her."

"And what exactly are you going to do to stop me? Hmm? I mean, really—how can you protect a dead woman?"

I realized he wasn't talking about Alex and he continued, "Look, I'm here for reasons that don't have shit to do with you, so stay the fuck out of it, okay? She's not the elegant woman she pretends to be. She made my life hell and I aim to return the favor. Get rid of her and you'll never see me again."

I stared at him, speechless.

"You have my word. But if you don't," he looked around the property. "You've done some nice things to this place. I might just stick around for a while—your choice."

My shoulders relaxed. He tilted his head from side to side and said, "See you around," before vanishing.

I walked into the house to use the bathroom. When I finished, I walked out of the bathroom to another surprise. Sara stood in the middle of the living room.

"What the hell did he want?" she said defiantly.

"He wants you out," I said.

"I'm not going anywhere."

She walked past me and out the door, stood on the patio and shouted, "DARYL. COME BACK, YOU COWARD!"

He appeared out of nowhere and stood face to face with her. She never faltered. She stood strong and said, "I hate you, you bastard."

He leaned closer and said, "How can you hate me?" then shouted, "YOU FUCKING CREATED ME," and suddenly vanished again.

I stood, shocked at what I was seeing. Sara was standing her ground. She portrayed confidence instead of a scared girl cowering to his commands. In addition, she was outside; something she's never been able to do since the night Daryl shot her. I kept staring at her as the breeze blew her hair lightly off her shoulder. She looked over at me and her confidence faded just as her apparition did. Before she disappeared, she reached her hand out through the open door.

Chapter 14

The Letter

Alex

Tuesday, July 9th 10:17 PM

You awake?

I sat in my recliner and stared at the phone, touching the screen occasionally to keep it active. Five minutes after I sent the message, she read it. Soon after, I saw the dots flash, and she replied with, 'YES.' I questioned sending the next message. If I did, would she stay away and *never* come back to Tennessee at all? That was irrational. She had her business and referring clients. I didn't build up a dramatic story, I replied with,

Daryl's Back

She read it instantly. I could only imagine what was going on in her mind.

Are you sure?

Positive

How can you be certain?

I talked to him

I'll be home late tomorrow.

You don't have to leave early, Alex. Do what you need to do at your conference. I'm not going anywhere. Besides, flight change fees will be ridiculous.

She read it but didn't reply—again. I wondered if she was close to the airport. Was she in the city of Dallas or a suburb around it? I set my phone on the arm of the chair as a thought entered my mind.

I had to go pick her up at Rick's when she was too drunk to drive home. I called her and made her share her location with me.

I pulled up the locations app and waited as it searched for Alex. The dot appeared on the screen and the map refreshed. I used my fingers to zoom out and saw she was in, what looked like, a small town called Russiaville.

I zoomed out more and I saw the surrounding cities; Kokomo, Frankfort, Lebanon and—*what the hell?* Indianapolis.

Although I knew little of her childhood, Anna shared many stories with me of her teenage years; her years at Western High School—in Russiaville, Indiana.

I held the phone in my left hand and rubbed my forehead with my right, resting my elbow on the arm of the chair with my eyes closed. I placed the phone on the seat beside me. My mind was void of any thoughts. I lifted my head and looked around the living room aimlessly. For the previous few weeks, I had seen ghosts move around as if they were right there beside me. One of them was Alex's grandfather telling me to protect her. Alex had been acting strange, staring at her phone since before my friends came to visit, asking a lot of questions about Anna. Daryl was back and wanted Sara out of the house, and I had just received new information that left me questioning everything. The conference Alex went to in Dallas wasn't in Dallas at all. She was in Anna's old hometown in Indiana that I had never spoken of.

I scrolled through the text messages with Alex and stopped on the one from Sunday night. She said to trust her and that she would explain everything when she came home. She would be home late the next day. I considered asking Sara more questions, but decided she wouldn't say anything anyway and it would only serve to piss me off that much more.

I reclined the chair all the way back, interlocked my hands behind my head and stared at the ceiling.

Where's the connection?

I dozed in the chair, so I got up to take a shower before laying down for the night. Every sound in the house made me feel like I did the first night I stayed there. I rushed to get clean and turned the water off so there was as little noise as possible when I got into bed.

Floor creaks sounded like chainsaws, squeaks sounded like metal scraping metal and the buzz of the refrigerator was like an air-raid siren.

"This isn't what we imagined, Anna. I'm sorry, honey. I should have kept looking. You deserve better."

I laid on my left side, placed my hands under my face and curled my feet up.

> *"Hi Sweetheart," she said.*
>
> *"Hi Baby. Why are you here, Anna?"*
>
> *"For you; to let you know it's all going to be okay. Toby, you can't let anyone ruin this for us. This is our place. Our forever house, and I love it."*
>
> *I reached my hand out and pushed my fingers through her long, blonde hair. She smiled at me. "I love you, Mister Miller."*
>
> *"I love you too, Annaliese."*

The next morning, I woke up to a sunny day but stayed in bed with thoughts racing through my mind like leaves in a cyclone. Sometimes, one would stop long enough to cause emotional pain and, other times, the thoughts left so fast, I did not know what they were.

I sent a message to Alex asking if she was coming to my place, if I was going over there or if we would meet somewhere; and asked her when. Twenty minutes later, she replied that she'd be at my house by 6:00 that evening. I sent one last message to her; "Drive safely," to which I received no response.

I did my typical morning routine, sitting on the back porch with coffee. It was 8:38 AM. I sipped my coffee and replayed the events with Daryl in my mind from the night before as if some holographic video was playing in my backyard. It seemed like thirty minutes had passed when I looked at my phone again. It was 8:42 AM and I knew it would be one of the longest days of my life.

I did what I could to keep myself busy all day, including moving the computer desk back into the office and putting the bed into the basement. I washed, dried and put away all of my laundry, cleaned every dish in the house, dusted every surface and vacuumed the floor —twice.

I looked out the office window obsessively at a quarter past five, in case she had left early or was making good time. I had just poured my second beverage when I heard the tires on the gravel drive. I walked through the galley and stood to the side of the kitchen window, peering out to see how she acted. When she turned the car off, she gathered things into her purse that was sitting on the passenger seat. It looked like a power cord for her phone, a tube of lipstick, some loose cash and change, and an envelope.

"Awe, a card. How fucking thoughtful," I said under my breath.

She pulled her purse onto her lap and pulled down the visor to use the mirror; pressing her lips together and baring her teeth after rubbing her tongue along the front edge behind her upper lip. She sighed and appeared to be taking deep breaths. She looked at her car mirrors, down at the floor, over to the passenger side, up at my house and started the cycle over with her car mirrors. Twice, she reached for the car door but didn't open it. She ran her hands through her hair, took another deep breath and opened the door when her shoulders dropped, toting only her purse. I raced into the living room so she wouldn't know I was watching her.

When she knocked on the door, I took a few controlled breaths behind the stone wall by the fireplace, then trudged to the front door. I unlocked the deadbolt, then the handle and opened it without saying a word. I gestured for her to come in. She offered a fake, sheepish smile that reflected embarrassment. When she got all the way into the kitchen, I closed the door behind her and offered her a drink.

"Yes, please," she said as though she was a stranger.

My heart was beating fast, and she sighed several times until I handed her the beverage.

"I'm not sure how to begin, Toby," she said.

"Why don't you start by telling me why you keep lying? Alex, if we're going to continue, we have to trust each other and right now, I'm not sure I can do that."

She reached both of her hands out and I accepted with both of mine. She looked into my eyes. "I know, and I am so—sorry for that. I didn't know how to tell you."

"That you weren't in Dallas at all? Fuck, Alex, that's easy. You just had to tell me where you were really going."

She looked away when tears fell and I continued, "You've been acting strange for weeks. You're obsessed with your phone, you've been asking about Anna, and yesterday, I find out that you're in the little town where she grew up. Why don't you start there? What are you looking for and why?"

"Can we sit at the table?"

I let go of her hands and walked into the dining room without speaking. She reached into her purse and pulled out a blank envelope. She breathed deeply a few times and tapped the envelope on the table before opening the flap.

"Toby," she started. "Saturday night, after you left, I watched some of your family videos. Your wedding was beautiful and wow," she laughed. "I could tell how hot it was that day. Your pictures of the mountains are beautiful and the way you sync the pictures to the music is really amazing." She rubbed a single finger along the rim of her glass and stared at it. "You were so happy together."

My anger faded into sadness and confusion. I did not understand why any of it mattered.

"When I watched the one from the following year; something specific caught my attention. She bought you a card for your anniversary. It was so sweet."

"It was red," I said. "With silver print on it."

"Yes."

"I don't remember every word, but it was something about our worlds joining into one and how I was her rock. She signed it with TODAY, TOMORROW and FOREVER, Anna."

"That's the one," she said.

"What about it?" I asked.

She pulled the hand-written letter out of the envelope, unfolded it and turned it to face me at the same time as she asked, "Toby, do you recognize this handwriting?"

I covered my mouth with my hand. I couldn't believe what I was seeing. "Oh God, that's Anna's handwriting."

"You're positive?"

"Yes, her handwriting was unique. I've never seen anyone write even similar to her—where did you get that?"

That's when her own tears fell. She sobbed as she handed me the letter. "I got it in the mail back in January. I never put it together until I saw the video with the close-up of the anniversary card and immediately recognized the writing."

I unfolded the letter and imagined Anna's voice as I read.

Dear Miss Reagan,

I'm sure this may be the strangest letter you've ever received, just as it's the strangest one I've ever written. I don't know how to say this, but I'm going to try my best.

My mother was very young when I was born. She was 16 when she got pregnant, 17 when I was born. My grandparents didn't approve, so she hid that she was pregnant as long as she could, wearing larger clothes as she got bigger. When she felt like she couldn't hide it anymore, she ran away until I was born and gave me up for adoption. Mom went back home, never expecting to say a word about me to anyone ever again, but was guilt-ridden and told her parents the truth. Her actions disgusted them and she was forbidden to return to their home, so she ran away again.

She contacted the state to regain custody but failed. As she explained it the only time we spoke, which was a few years ago, she got multiple jobs and supported herself and fell in love a year later. A year after that, she got married, but kept her own legal name. Ten months later, Mom gave birth again. This is where it really gets weird and I don't know how to say it, so I'm just going to put it out there. Alex, my Mom gave birth to twins girls. I was born a Reagan in Tennessee, but was adopted by the people I know now as my parents who changed my legal name to Lindley. We lived most *of my life in Russiaville, Indiana. My mother died a few years ago, and I never found out the name of my father.*

My husband, Toby, and I would like to live in the mountains of Tennessee someday and I came across your name on a realtor's website. I received your business card in the mail last week and would love nothing more than to meet my sisters. I can't explain why I'm so confident it's you, but I am.

I hope this letter finds you and Seraphina well and I know this is a lot to take in. If you want to talk, I've included my business card. Feel free to call at any time.

Sincerely,

Anna Miller

I stopped reading several times to regain my composure. I alternated between looking at the letter and looking at the table, or out the sliding glass door behind Alex. "Did you ever call her?"

She cried harder. "No," she said through sobs. "With Sara dead, I couldn't bear to replace her. I tried to dismiss it, but I couldn't. Toby, I've probably read this letter a hundred times and it never clicked until I saw Anna's hand-writing on your family video. I wondered if she might be the same; that's why I kept asking questions about her childhood. When I watched the video, I couldn't bear the thought I've lost both of my sisters. That's why I left on Monday morning. Toby, I'm so sorry."

I wiped tears off my face with a napkin from the table and laughed.

"What could possibly be funny?" she asked.

I looked into her glossy, tear-filled hazel eyes and said, "I'm in love with my sister-in-law."

She smiled through her tears and said, "What did you say?"

I stood up and took her into my arms when she stood too. "I love you, Alex. I love you. I missed you this week and I'm sorry I got mad."

"I love you too, Toby. I never meant for this to happen."

"How could you? This might just be the biggest series of coincidental events I've ever heard of."

"I never knew a person could cry so much as I have the past few days. The three of us would have had so much fun together," she said; "Anna, Sara and I."

We stood quietly for a moment, holding each other. She let go and I did the same. She asked, "Do you mind if I change the subject for a minute?"

"No, I don't mind at all."

"You said Daryl's back. What happened?"

"The storms were terrible Sunday night and most of the day on Monday."

I told her every detail about the storms, what I saw Sunday night and the interaction with Daryl the previous night. She looked worried, a little scared and somewhat confused when she asked me, "What did he want?"

I looked around the house, thinking of Sara. "You up for a ride in the park?" I asked.

"I'm always up for a ride in the park."

Chapter 15

The Ghost Beside Us

I gathered my camera equipment and loaded the Sorento before we left. When we got to US-321 towards Greenbrier, she asked again, "What does Daryl want?"

"He wants Sara gone. He said if we get rid of her, we'll never see him again."

"Why?"

"He told me she made his life hell and that his goal was to do the same thing to her."

"I'm not doing a damn thing that man says, Toby."

I didn't respond to her. I made a left turn before reaching the Parkway and took the Baskins Creek Bypass to Cherokee Orchard Road to get to the Motor Nature Trail.

"What are you thinking, Mister?" she asked.

"I'm not so sure that's a good idea; not doing what he says."

"Keep going, I'm listening."

"She's living out a punishment; her version of Hell as far as we can tell. She stayed behind because she believed she deserved it, right?"

"Yeah, I guess. You're the one who talks to her all the time."

"She cowered to him. She was scared of him. We want peace for her, right?"

"Of course."

"If peace for her means crossing over—if it means she's not stuck here anymore, afraid of her own shadow, then I believe we don't have a choice. Ultimately, you, me and Daryl want the same thing for Sara, but for different reasons."

"Toby, I just *hate* for him to believe he got something he wanted from being a dickhead."

"You're saying you'd rather try to teach him a lesson than see your sister at peace?"

"That makes me sound like a bad person."

"Alex, all I'm saying is that Daryl wants her out of the house. Maybe she's protected by us somehow so he can't do what he really wants unless she's out of the house. I don't know. I'm not going to pretend I have any clue what the hell that psycho is thinking. If she crosses over, she'll be at peace, which is what we want for her. She'll be out of the house and he won't be able to torment her."

"I will not be nice to that bastard."

"You don't have to be. He wants her out and he'll leave for good. He'll probably just move on to mess with somebody else, but at least we'll be rid of him."

"And how do you propose we help her cross over?"

"I'm not so sure we need to do much more than we already are."

"What do you mean?" she asked.

"Remember when you told her you want peace for her and she said you don't get to choose what her peace is?"

"Yes."

"She vanished again, right?"

"Yes, like she always does."

"I agree, she vanishes all the time, but it wasn't like she always does. It was different that time. She didn't vanish because she wanted to. She had her hands up and looked at them as if it surprised her she was fading. It happened again the other night."

"She showed herself again?" she asked, surprised.

"Yes; even stood up to Daryl. They stood nose-to-nose. She told him she hated him. Right after she stood up to him, she faded again, like she did with you. And like before, she reached out her hand before she vanished."

"What does all of that mean, Toby?"

"I think it means, she's finding inner peace. Once she believes in herself, she'll stop believing she deserves this and she'll have no reason to stay."

I saw her look out the window as we approached the Park Vista and the access to the Nature Trail. I put my hand on hers, “What is it?”

“Then she’ll be gone.”

I looked back out the window as I navigated the curves in the road and empathized when I said, “Yes, she will.”

As I recalled the confrontation in my mind, I remembered something else. “He said something else too, but I don’t know what it means.”

“What did he say?”

“Before he vanished, he said to her, 'How can you hate me when you created me?' What does that mean?”

“It’s his victim bullshit. He blames her for the way he is. Toby, what if he’s lying? What if Sara crosses over and he still doesn’t leave?”

“I say we both need to brush up on our skills.”

“What do you mean?”

“If he stays, we must find a way to communicate with him on our terms. I’ll book an investigation and we’ll learn everything we can.”

She smiled and said, “I’d like that.”

I pulled her hand up to kiss it and said, “I’m sure glad you’re back.”

“Me too. I don’t like Indiana. It’s too flat.”

“Don’t say that out loud to the locals. They love it.”

“I gathered that. They’re proud of their home state.”

“Yes, they are.”

We turned off Cherokee Orchard Road and onto the single lane Motor Nature Trail past the parking area for Rainbow Falls.

"You ever been to Rainbow Falls?" she asked.

"No. That was one that Anna always said was a short hike but was rated as being difficult only to reach a dry waterfall. It's all about the timing with some of these waterfalls. Some of them, you really need a good water flow, while others, like Spruce Flats, look better with less water."

When we reached the nature trail, I lowered all the windows, opened the sunroof and maintained the five miles per hour speed limit. There was a car approaching behind me, so I let him go by at the next pull-off. I parked, turned to Alex and changed the subject, "Hey, how are you doing?"

"Me? I'm fine, why?"

"You just learned about Anna. I can't imagine what's going through your mind right now; knowing you had another sister you never met."

"I don't know, Toby. I don't know what to think other than wanting to watch the rest of those videos. Hopefully, I'll learn at least something about my big sister."

No other cars were approaching, so I pulled onto the driving trail again. "What did you find out when you were in Indiana?"

"Nothing. I tried to go to her old school but I couldn't reach anyone. I didn't have any luck at the historical society either. Mostly, it was a wasted trip."

I drove the switchbacks of the winding road along the side of Mount LeConte. As we rounded a bend to the right, I made sure no one was behind me and stopped in the middle of the road.

"Look!" I exclaimed when I saw the unmistakable dark mass of a black bear that moseyed across the woods with its head down, looking for food. I pulled over and we watched him for several minutes. When he walked away, down a hill and out of sight, I pulled back onto the road.

"That will never get old," I said. "Sorry I interrupted. You were saying it was a wasted trip. What did you do all week?"

"There are several little parks I drove to, and walked around, wondering if Anna ever did the same."

"I don't know. She never mentioned it. Her goal in life as a teenager was to get out of that small town and live in the city. Living within the city limits, things are fast-paced. We felt like our life was going by too fast, which is why we wanted to move down here."

I pulled off at a few places that Anna and I stopped at several times to tell Alex stories about my wife; her sister. We laughed at some tales and others, we didn't.

We rounded the other side of the mountain where the road follows Roaring Fork. The water roared along the creeks from the storms of the previous two days and the cascades were beautiful, but it was getting dark, so we didn't stop often.

Toward the end of the Motor Nature Trail, I stopped at a place I had been to so many times—Reagan's Mill. I pulled into a parking space across from the small mill and held her hand as we walked down to the shallow bank of Roaring Fork. The water raced by us as we stood behind the old mill; an amazing view of the scene hanging on my living room wall and that I posted on my photography website called *Behind the Mill.*

The headlights from the other cars blinded us as they came down the hill towards the mill. When one car passed, she took her cell phone out and laid her head on my shoulder with the water flowing behind us, raised the camera up a little and she snapped the picture.

"Wow, that's a pretty decent picture," she said.

I smiled when I looked at it. "Will you please send it to me? I believe that's the first picture of you and I together."

She leaned over and kissed me before walking back to the truck to head home.

When we picked up US-321 again, she said, "Toby, I'm sorry."

"For what?"

"For lying to you. For keeping things from you." She was silent for a moment until she asked, "Are we okay?"

"From now on, we do things together. No secrets or we won't be okay. Fair?" I asked.

"That's fair, yes."

"Then, yes, we're okay."

She grinned and asked, "Did you just get mad at me?"

"No, I was mad at you earlier in the week. That was setting my boundaries, not being mad."

When we pulled up in front of the house, Alex unbuckled her seatbelt and said, "I think I'm officially sick of being in a car for today."

"You can stay if you'd like," I offered.

I hadn't finished the statement when she jumped a little and replied with, "Okay"

I laughed when I said, "Did you just hop?"

She looked from side to side with her eyes, nodded her head and giggled, "Yep, I think I did."

I unlocked the front door, walked into the dark house, reached my arm out to the wall and flipped the light switch.

"I wonder where Sara is," she asked.

I remembered one other thing I needed to tell Alex. I leaned close to Alex's ear and whispered, "There's something else I need to tell you about Sara. Do you mind stepping back outside?"

"Why do we keep going outside?"

"Because she can't follow us out here. Look, she might ask you something and I'm not at all comfortable with it."

"Okay, what is it?"

"Sara admitted that she has feelings for me. She likes to experiment to see what she can feel and what I can feel."

She shook her head in disbelief.

"The other day, she tried to blackmail me. She said she knew what you were up to and I was getting desperate to know the truth. She said she'd tell me if I talked you into allowing her to touch me."

"What? Are you serious?"

"Yes, I'm afraid I am. She said she could feel me that day when you were talking in the living room."

"She could feel you because she fucking possessed me."

I put my hands up in front of me and said, “Alex, don’t get mad at me. I’m only being honest and telling you what happened and what she said.”

“I’m not mad at you. I just can’t believe she actually thinks I would let her—that I would allow her to—*damn*, that girl’s got a nerve.”

“Watch your back, okay? She did it before without you knowing.”

“You had sex with my sister?”

“Oh, God no! All I'm saying is she possessed you before without you knowing.”

She put her arms back down to her sides after crossing them and I took a step towards the door.

“Oh, Alex?”

“Yes?”

“I was married to Anna, so technically, I did have sex with your sister.”

She smiled and said, “*Half*-sister, Tobias. She’s just a half-sister.”

Both of us were tired when we walked back into the house. She showered after me and sat on the couch in pajamas. I got my laptop out and sat it on my legs on the couch. “Let’s find a place to investigate.”

“Ooh, this is exciting,” Alex said and ran over to sit next to me.

“Do you want to stay close?”

“I don’t care. I mean, I don’t want to go too far. Somewhere we can drive to but not take all day to get there.”

“Let’s see what’s close.”

I pulled up a search engine and typed in 'HAUNTED PLACES NEAR GATLINBURG', which returned several results. 'HAUNTED PLACES NEAR KNOXVILLE', 'HAUNTED PLACES NEAR PIGEON FORGE'; all of them provided results, but nothing as active as I hoped for. We skimmed over several more haunted places for half an hour before Alex asked, "Is there anywhere you and Anna wanted to go, but never got the chance?"

I looked over to her without expression.

"I'm sorry, Toby, does that upset you?"

"No," I said calmly. "There is a place. It's considered one of the most haunted places in the world; Callosity Sanitarium, in Louisville."

I searched to see how far Louisville was from my house. It was almost five hours.

"Let's do it," I said.

"When?"

"Now, tomorrow—we'll call in the morning to see when they have tickets."

"Sounds good," Alex said through a yawn.

"I'm tired too," I said. "Ready to lie down?"

"Yes, I am, Mister."

Alex walked straight into the master bedroom and laid down while I walked around the house to turn off the lights, leaving only the night lights on. I walked to the front door and locked my Sorento with the fob, hung the keys back on the hook and laid in bed.

Alex curled right up next to me. The sheets were cool when we got in them so we rubbed each other's arms for warmth. Once we got comfortable, I relaxed. Alex rubbed my chest with her fingertips, then kissed my arm, then my chest.

I whispered, “I thought you were tired.”

“Not too tired for this,” she said sensually.

She slowly draped her leg over me and lifted herself until she was sitting on my upper thighs. I watched her as she rubbed her hands across the back of her neck and pulled all of that beautiful hair over one of her shoulders, then kept rubbing my chest with both hands. She shivered—then stopped moving.

“Sara, where are you?” she asked.

“I’m right here—beside you—as always.”

Chapter 16

Scarred

"Get out!" Alex scolded then laid against me under the covers. She pulled her hands up to her chest, draped her leg across mine and she shivered until she got warm.

We laid on our backs without talking. Alex lifted her head occasionally to look around the room and out the French Doors.

"Damn her," she said.

I had my hand around her back and rubbed her arm until she relaxed. As I laid there, I woke up several times without knowing I had even fallen asleep. Each time I woke was from Alex turning onto either side, or onto her back. She turned onto her stomach with one leg pulled up and her arm around a pillow.

I whispered, "You still awake?"

"Yes."

"You okay? You keep tossing."

"Why didn't she tell me, Toby?"

"About her feelings for me?"

"No, I'm talking about my mother. Why the hell didn't she ever tell us we had a big sister?"

"What was your Mom's name?" I asked.

"Josephine. Daddy was Stephen. It's like my whole life has been a lie."

She rolled onto her side with her elbow on the bed and rested the side of her head onto her hand. "I keep thinking of when we were little, you know? I'm trying to think of early memories and to remember conversations. Did she ever try to tell us? Were there ever any hints?"

"Were there any?"

"None. Not one. Not that I know of, anyway."

I let her recall memories without interrupting and she continued, "Everyone treated Sara and I like we were different in school. We were the Reagan Twins and got a lot of attention we didn't like. We wanted a baby brother or sister. I remember being at the dinner table. Sara told me I shouldn't, but I asked anyway. I said, 'why didn't you have another baby?' She could have said it then, but didn't."

"How old were you?"

"Eight or nine."

"That's kind of young to tell you, don't you think?"

"Maybe, but that night, she knew we wanted a little brother or sister. She could have told us as we got older. Nothing, Toby. Neither of them ever said a word about it."

"What about your grandmother? You said your grandpa died before you were born; did you get to know your grandmother?"

She laughed and said, "No, other than Granny pinching my cheeks."

"She pinched your cheeks?"

"All the time. Every time we'd see her and when we left. I was really little then; that's all I remember."

"What about your other grandparents; on your Mom's side?"

"We never saw them. As children, we *had* grandparents. Granny pinched my cheeks and I never met Papaw. When we were old enough to realize we should have had two sets of grandparents, we asked about them. Momma only told us they were mean people and she didn't want us around them."

"Alex, even you said everyone has secrets, right? Maybe that was one she just didn't know how to tell you, or was too painful for her."

She thought about it for a moment, looked into my eyes and said, "Maybe you're right," and put her head on the pillow again.

"Toby. Toby, sweetie—Tobias!"

When I woke up, Alex set a cup of coffee on my nightstand.

"Mm, coffee," I mumbled.

She walked around the house and talked non-stop. When her voice got louder, I looked through the French doors as she walked in and said, "What do you think?"

"About what?"

"Did you hear a word I said?"

I stretched with a growl and said, "Yes, of course, I did. You asked me what I think."

She laughed and said, "I mean, before that, you dope."

I smiled because it was the only option I had, considering the real answer was that I did *not* hear a single word she said.

"I got tickets to the place in Louisville this morning."

"Oh, cool. When do we go?"

She smiled with a wink, "You really didn't hear anything, did you?"

I looked down and said, "No, ma'am, I did not."

"Their private tours and investigations are booked until mid-September. October is full, too. We have tickets for the public tour tonight."

"Tonight?" I asked.

"Yes. Tonight means it's the same day we're in now, but later, when the sun sets and before we go to bed."

"Smart ass."

Her smile diminished when I sipped my coffee.

"Toby?"

"Yes, dear."

"What's it like being in a real haunted building? I know what we've been through. Will it be like that all the time?"

"Oh, God, no—I sure as hell hope not, anyway. Each place is a little different. Most start with the history of the place. Sometimes, they have equipment with them and other times, it's just a tour. Did you see anything online about that?"

"No."

I took another sip of my coffee as my mind shifted. "I wonder if —" I looked outside through the sliding door.

"If what?"

"If I'll see them," I said, still gazing towards the backyard. "This —gift I have. I don't know how it will affect me this time. I've done investigations before, but before the night of Anna's accident, I had only seen an apparition one time."

"You having second thoughts?"

"Of course, I am. They're not going to change my mind though."

I looked towards Alex again, who was still standing in the doorway. "Alex, we *have* to get rid of him."

We each packed an overnight bag, loaded them into the truck and were on our way by 11:00. Alex fell asleep before we reached Knoxville. The route we took was the same to get to Indianapolis until reaching Lexington, Kentucky, where we stopped to fill the gas tank. Alex woke up only long enough to ask where we were and fell right back to sleep. She didn't even wake up when I started the SUV and got back onto the interstate.

Gifted. What will I feel? What will I see, and who? Protect her. From what? From whom? Was it even Alex I was supposed to protect?

The longer I drove, the more I felt like I was driving into a battle; a battle against the paranormal, yes, but mostly, a battle within my mind. Madame Rose believed I was gifted.

If you want to develop the gift, you must first accept it.

Had I accepted it? Is that the reason I saw them so much? Why did I see the couple at the bend along the Little River, Alex's grandfather in her office, or the veteran at the parade?

I saw a sign for a rest area, pulled in and tried to wake Alex when I settled into a parking space.

"Alex. Alex," I said as I gently shook her leg.

"Yes."

"We're at a rest area. Do you need to go in?"

She sighed, turned towards the window and fell back to sleep. I locked the truck when I walked inside, wondering if she slept at all the night before.

She woke up when we got back onto the interstate and said, "Where are we?"

"We're getting close to Frankfort. Are you okay?"

She opened her eyes wide, stretched and said, "Yeah, I'm okay. Just tired."

"Did you sleep at all last night?"

"A little, but I kept waking up. It was more like taking a bunch of naps than it was sleeping. How much further is it?"

"A little more than an hour. Do you need anything?"

"I'm getting hungry, but if it's only an hour, I can wait until we get there."

When I was back up to full speed, I set the cruise control again and started a conversation. I wondered how Alex imagined the investigation would be.

"What's on your mind? I remember going on my first investigation. We were really excited, but I was also a little scared. Do you have any thoughts about what it's going to be like?"

I looked into my mirror and merged into the next lane to pass the driver in front of me.

"Alex?"

She fell asleep again. I put my hand on her leg and smiled. Her arms were curled into her chest. The temperature control setting was the same on both sides, so I pushed the button to separate them and turned up the temperature on the passenger side.

I saw her leg flinch out of my peripheral vision and smiled again. She moaned. I put my hand back on her leg and rubbed it with my thumb. She relaxed and licked her lips, so I returned my focus to the road.

Her leg flinched again, then her arm, then her leg again. She moved her head from side to side. I put my hand on the back of her neck and said, "Alex, honey, wake up. You're dreaming."

She screamed and sat forward in her seat with her arms in her lap. Her arms and legs were tense as she continued to scream. My instincts took over and I looked out the windshield and at every mirror within seconds. Traffic hadn't stopped anywhere. I looked over to Alex who was still screaming.

"ALEX!" I yelled and rubbed her back, alternating my attention between her and the road ahead.

She stopped screaming, relaxed and looked at me.

"Holy shit, Alex, you scared the shit out of me."

"I'm sorry, I had a bad dream."

My heart was racing, and I raised my shoulders with both hands on the steering wheel. Still trying to catch my breath, I asked her if she could reach the cooler in the back to hand me a soft drink.

She rubbed her eyes and shook her head, then unbuckled her seat belt and turned around to get two beverages out of the cooler.

"Jesus, what did you dream about?"

She was breathing fast too. She turned around, opened my soft drink, put her seat belt back on, and reached her hand out. I relaxed my shoulders and held her hand. She looked out the window and said, "Toby, it felt real."

"What did? What was the dream?"

"Sara," she said.

"Sara? What about her?"

She didn't answer right away. Instead, she gazed out the side window. She dropped her head and shook it back and forth in disbelief and sighed several times.

I pulled her hand up to my mouth and kissed it. "Alex, what happened?"

"I was dancing in the living room; your living room, only, it was set up the same way it was when Sara lived there. There was a man—a young man twirling me around and we were laughing. He stopped spinning and pulled me towards him and kissed me. There was a noise outside, and we both looked towards the door, then ran. I escorted him down to the basement. We were scared. I told him to run out the back door and around the garage to hide. When I turned around, Daryl was already coming down the stairs, yelling, 'whose fucking truck is out front?' He stormed up to me and stood an inch from my face and screamed, 'I asked you a question, Sara.'"

"Sara?"

"Yes, it wasn't me in the dream. It was as if I was seeing it happen as Sara."

"That's weird. Is that what made you scream?"

"No, that was just the beginning. He looked past me and saw the young man running around the garage and pushed me out of the way to get to him. He slid the door open and chased after him. I cried and screamed, 'NO' to him, but he never stopped. As he turned the corner around the back of the garage, the other man was on the opposite corner on the front right and looked at me. I waved my hand and yelled for him to run. He sprinted across the open area and around the front of the house. His truck started and he revved it twice. I heard his tires spinning on the gravel. Daryl ran from around the garage and after the truck, but the man sped off behind the trees. Sara went—no, I went back into the basement and up the stairs. When I reached the top of the stairs, he was coming through the front door. I stopped at the opening to the kitchen, he looked at me with tears in his eyes and said, 'How could you do this to me?' as he walked into the living room. I followed him, but pulled a knife out of the drawer in the galley kitchen."

"Oh, shit, Alex. You said you were Sara the whole time?"

"Yes."

"I bet that was weird."

"Toby, in the dream, I pulled the knife up and stabbed him in the shoulder with it as he walked away."

"He probably deserved it, if it were me having a dream like that, I'd probably wake up laughing."

"It wasn't like that. We were younger. The feeling I got in the dream—as Sara—wasn't vengeance, it was malicious. Daryl was the scared one in my dream, not Sara."

"Was that the whole dream?"

"No, after that, it was like the dream skipped forward to the night of our fight. I told him I felt like a prisoner in my home and that I was going out with my sister and told him there was nothing he could do about it."

"Wow. Isn't that what happened, that night?"

"Yes. The next thing was when he stood in the galley kitchen with a pistol aimed. When he fired the shot, I screamed as I watched the bullet spinning towards me. That's when I woke up."

"That is one crazy dream. I've had those before where it's almost like it's real, and I never forget them."

"Toby," she said, looking at me again.

"Yeah."

"I saw Daryl without a shirt one time in my life. He had a two-inch scar on the back of his right shoulder. He was working on his truck in the garage before their relationship got bad. When he saw me looking at his shoulder, he put his shirt back on."

"Alex, that doesn't mean anything. You know about the scar and your mind made up some version of how it happened. Did you ever ask him about it?"

"No, he was uncomfortable already, so I didn't want to bring more attention to it."

I imagined the events happening as she explained them. I opened my mouth to comment when she said, "What if it wasn't just a dream? What if I recalled a memory of something that happened, but I never saw?"

She shifted to take my right hand into both of hers and said, "Toby, what if it was real?"

Chapter 17

Callosity

We arrived at our hotel after 4:00, collected trash from the Sorento and settled into our fourth-floor room. Neither Alex nor I spoke of her dream the rest of the trip. *What if she's right?* I thought. What if she had a vision of the past from Sara's perspective? Twins have a different connection. If her dream served no other purpose, it made me question Sara's integrity, her intentions, and her character. I heard Daryl's voice in my mind.

She's not the elegant woman she pretends to be. She made my life hell.

Based on my experience, I classified Daryl as a strong, controlling, egotistical, bully. Regardless of how I classified him, I couldn't dismiss the possibility he told the truth.

We laid on the bed and napped until my alarm woke us up at 6:30, not knowing how long that evening's investigation would last. When we awoke, we freshened up and drove to a small diner nearby for supper.

"You don't seem all that excited," I said.

"Honestly, I'm getting a little nervous."

"There's nothing to be nervous about. I've only done this a few times, but when I have, it's been really interesting. You may hear things or get cold chills. We can take pictures on our phones to capture orbs when they tell us stories of things that have happened in the place. It's pretty cool because if you capture an orb in a place that something happened, you've got a hell of a story to tell."

"And a picture to go with it," she added.

"Exactly. I'll have to show you some of what I've captured before."

"Honestly, Toby, I'm a little nervous for you, too."

I knew what she was talking about without her explaining it. The thought of seeing entities had been on my mind since Alex told me about the investigation that morning.

We finished our meals and paid our bill. When we got to the truck, I opened Alex's door for her, got into the driver's seat and entered the address in the navigation system.

The drive to Callosity was quiet. We pulled into a long drive, ending with a small, twenty-car parking lot on an incline. There were several cars parked in front of an access road with a 'NO TRESPASSING' sign mounted to a tall, hinged iron gate. We watched people laughing outside their vehicles while others pulled into the parking lot after we backed into a space with our windows down. We peered along the access road to see the building, but a line of trees blocked our view.

Twenty minutes later, silence spread across the parking lot when an overweight man approached from the other side of the gate in a golf cart, but didn't get out. He spoke into a two-way radio; too far away for the rest of us to hear.

Others got out of their vehicles and milled around the parking lot and occasionally glanced at the man.

"What is he doing?" Alex muttered.

It was 8:38 when I replied, "I don't know. What time is it supposed to start?"

She pulled the tickets out of her purse, scanned them and said, "8:30."

The sun was low in the Northern Kentucky sky, sinking behind wispy pink, yellow and orange clouds. A light breeze blew across the truck in through Alex's window and out mine. Commotion stirred in the parking lot, which got our attention. We turned our heads to see the man in the golf cart turn around and drive up the access road, beyond the tree line and out of sight. A minute later, he returned with a tall, skinny man on the other side. They stopped and the tall man exited the cart with a ring of keys. He was a cheerful man; slender with short, dark hair. He walked up to the gate and announced, "We're going to walk from here. No vehicles allowed past this point.

Secure your vehicles and, when we're all together, we'll walk up to check in. You might want to grab a light jacket. It'll be chilly when the sun goes down."

He unlocked the gate and walked it open. The high-pitched squeak ended with a bang when the gate met a post in the ground.

I whispered, "That's not creepy," closed the front windows and joined the others. The golf cart driver turned around again and drove off behind the tree line.

One woman told the man she was with, "I hope we have the same guide as last time."

"Me too," he replied.

I asked, "You've been here before?"

He said, "Yes, about a year ago. They split us up into two groups. One guide was a woman and the other was a man. The man seemed like a bit of an asshole. A few people complained about him when we left, but *she* was awesome. She showed us around, kept us together, but at certain places, allowed us to venture out a little."

"That's cool. Thanks, man."

"This your first time?" he asked.

"First time here. I've been to other places though."

"If you're all ready, follow me," the slender man said.

Woods lined both sides of the narrow access road we walked up. The incline was gradual but longer than it looked. Part of the group was in front of us while others were behind. Alex and I kept looking at an angle to our left to catch a glimpse of the building, but the woods were thick. There was a large utility shed at the top of the access road to the right and we could see the break in the tree line to the left.

The group had spread out more than when we started and the ones in the front muttered to each other.

"Oh, Wow."

"Look at that place."

"It's bigger than I expected."

We approached the end of the woods line and the building came into sight with the sun setting behind it. It was a dilapidated four-story building that had two long wings extending at an angle from the flush center wall. There was no glass in the large openings where windows once were. A crouched, stone gargoyle sat atop each angle and corner. Light from the sunset didn't pass through the building as if there were no window openings on the back side. Despite the large openings, we couldn't see anything beyond the outside walls.

I stopped to take a picture with my cell phone when we got close enough to capture the building, but not so close it wouldn't fit in the frame.

"This place gives me the creeps," Alex said as she held onto my arm with both of her hands.

We walked beyond the main building to a smaller one off to the right side where the tour started. The slender man held the door for us with a smile as we walked into the large room. When the last of our group entered, he announced, "You'll check in at the table over there," and pointed to the corner. "You'll need your reservations out so we can check you off the list."

Alex pulled the folded reservations out of her small purse. The man continued, “That’s also where you’ll sign the waiver.”

“The waiver?” Alex asked.

“Yes,” the man said. “There are hundreds of stairs on our tour. The waiver releases Callosity of liability for those who aren’t healthy enough for all the stairs.”

He turned to the rest of the group and spoke louder, “Did everyone hear that? You’ll all need to sign a waiver of responsibility. There are hundreds of steps here at Callosity and everyone needs to be healthy enough to take them. Also, if you thought this was a haunted house with people dressed up and ready to jump out and scare you, you’ve come to the wrong place. Our building is truly haunted and we can’t be held responsible for the actions of our—residents, I’ll call them.”

As people signed in, they wandered around the gift shop to look at crystals, dowsing rods, t-shirts, and more Callosity merchandise.

A man spoke louder than the hum of the group, “If you want something to drink, do it now. Beverages are strictly forbidden in our building. Restrooms are over there, by the gift shop. We’ll get started in two minutes.”

“You okay?” I asked Alex.

“Yeah, I’m alright,” she said, although she was still looking around the room.

“Are you excited?”

“Toby, I’m not so sure what the hell I’ve gotten myself into here, but I’m a bit uneasy.”

I looked around to make sure no one else could overhear, leaned in and said, “There’s nothing here that will be as bad as what we’ve already been through. It's like I told you; orbs, cold chills, and weird feelings. That's all."

The loud man stood on a chair and announced, "Okay, let's get started. Make it easy on me tonight and separate yourselves into two even groups. One group will be here with me, Mark, and the other will be with the lovely Patty, over there." He pointed to his right and, remembering what the man said when we first started walking, Alex and I didn't hesitate to go towards Patty. She was a little short-haired lady I would guess to be in her early forties.

Mark announced again, "Now, for the rules. If you don't follow the rules, we will remove you immediately with no refund. Just get out."

I whispered to Alex, "That's one way to get people to listen to the rules."

"Yes, it is," she whispered back. "Now I see why those people said he's an asshole."

I smiled, held her hand and listened.

"Rule number one; stay with the group. If you get separated, you can easily get lost and trust me when I say, this is not the place you want to get lost in. Rule number two; stay with the group."

There was light laughter before he continued, "Cell phones; turn them off. Not airplane mode, not vibrate, not silent, turn—them—off. If you were hoping to take pictures, your luck has run out because it will be far too dark to take pictures in there, anyway. Like I said, food and drink aren't allowed in the building. There are no restrooms once we get started and," he turned to Patty who was smiling. "is there anything I'm forgetting?"

"No, I think you covered it."

Mark spoke up again, "Patty's group; you're starting in the East Wing and my group is starting in the West Wing. Have fun, everybody, and please watch out for each other."

We followed Patty outside and across a gravel drive to a one-story extension off the back of the East Wing. She stopped by a heavy steel door.

"Before we go inside, let me tell you a little about Callosity Asylum."

I spoke up, "Asylum? I thought it was a sanitarium."

"The sanitarium is half mile North of here."

"Oh—is this as active as the sanitarium?"

She smiled and said, "Why don't you ask me that again at the end of the tour?"

"I take that as a yes," I laughed.

"It's *very* active," she said

She gathered us closer to make sure we could hear, and so she didn't have to shout. We shuffled closer to her and she began the tour.

"Callosity Asylum opened in April 1926. Back then, the judicial system believed children who committed crimes weren't criminals and didn't deserve jail time. Juvenile prisons were scarce as they had only been around for twenty-seven years. Local officials believed when minors committed crimes, they were mentally unstable and could be redirected in an asylum, rather than in a detention center, as we call them now. Callosity has 320 rooms. By the summer of 1935, there were close to twelve hundred children here. If you're bad at math like I am, I'll tell you that's four kids in almost every room;

every one of them a criminal in a state that hadn't bought into the juvenile system yet."

Someone closer to Patty asked, "What kind of crimes did they commit?"

"Theft, robbery, assault—murder. They separated the children into age groups, but not by the severity of their crime. It was common for a thief to be in the same room as a murderer. The top two floors were for children aged fifteen to seventeen. The second floor was for ages twelve to fourteen. Half of the first floor was for children that were ten or eleven."

She stopped talking and looked at our faces. Alex spoke up, "Okay, I'll bite; and the other half of the bottom floor?"

Patty smiled and said, "Good observation. The rest of the first floor was for criminal children under ten years old."

A woman to our right asked, "How young was the youngest?"

"Eight. Can you believe it? Eight years old."

"That's disgusting," the woman said and walked out of the group. The man she was with followed her.

Patty called to them, "If you're leaving, please check out first." She turned her attention back to the group. "We typically lose one or two at the beginning like that. But you see, many of our *residents*, as we call them, aren't children at all. We think some are the parents of children that were patients, while others are the grown versions of the residents, themselves. Possibly, ones that were released, later died and came back in the afterlife."

"Why is it so haunted?" one man asked. "Did a lot of the kids die here?"

"The conditions here were the best in the country. There was a separate cafeteria on each floor, four shower rooms, and two playrooms—on each floor. Between 1935 and 1941, over six hundred children died here. Some were from fights here at the asylum, but many were medical overdoses from trying to keep the peace."

I looked away from Patty and up to the enormous building we were standing next to. I could see the wall at the end of the building, the back of the East Wing and part of the flush, center section. I flinched and Alex whispered, "What is it, Toby? What did you see?"

"It's not what I saw."

"Then what is it, honey?"

I stared at the center of the fourth floor. "It's what I see."

"Right now?"

"Yes."

"Honey, what is it?"

He was translucent; see-through, like Sara was sometimes. A boy who looked to be a teenager stood on the roof with his arms out, facing the back of the building. I didn't answer Alex.

"Patty?" I called out.

"Yes."

"Were there any documented suicides here?"

"Just one. Jimmy. He likes to hang out on the roof."

She scanned the group and said, "Ya'll ready to go in?"

There was an eerie silence. None of us spoke.

"I take that as a yes," she said. "When we get in here, it's really dark. It's a narrow passage. Stand along the opposite wall. I'll tell you about this place when we're all inside."

She unlocked the door and held it open for all of us to enter, then used the light on her cell phone to guide us inside. Alex and I were the last ones to go in. She pulled the door closed behind her and shined her light on the ground until she shuffled to the front of the group. When she turned it off, all light was gone. There were no lights along the hallway; no glowing phone faces, and no windows. I looked around the edge of the door we came through. Even as my eyes adjusted, the faintest sliver of light couldn't be seen. It made nighttime in Tennessee look like dusk.

"We're standing in an area they referred to as 'The Pit.' Basically, it was solitary confinement for repeated behavioral problems. When a child was sent here, they were only given crackers to eat and two glasses of water a day; one in the morning and one at night along with a caffeine pill. Do not go past me, for any reason. Directly past us, the floor drops at a steep angle into the underground confinement area. When this building was active, children coming out of solitary reported noises and things brushing up against them *inside* their confinement room. What they reported the most was a gravelly voice inside the room whispering to them. Most kids reported that the voice told them to do things that would get them in trouble, be it, stealing something or, even one report that a fifteen-year-old boy claimed the voice told him to kill a nurse."

The group muttered to each other. One lady asked, "Patty, do you know who the voice was?"

"There is no heat down there and some kids died after exposure to the cold. We think it might be Jimmy. I'll tell you more about him later, when we get to the observation room on the roof. Want to see down there? This is one place you may take flash pictures."

Cell phones came out from every person in the group, and the dank hallway was lit up all around us. We all leaned around each other to see the passage behind her. We took turns going to the front to take a photograph. When it was my turn, Alex stayed right behind me. The concrete hall led, at an angle, two stories down. The walls were visible along their full length, but even with the light of everyone's phones, there was no light penetrating the darkness beyond the end of the walls.

"Phones off again, please," Patty announced. She kept her light on and walked through the middle of the group, pointing the light at the ground. She stopped past us, turned around and said, "We're going to continue down this hallway and into the main building. Please stay together. This is your last chance to leave the group. There is no electricity anywhere in the building. Ladies and Gentlemen, Callosity isn't ranked as one of the most haunted buildings in the country for no reason. You *will* see, hear or feel some of our residents along the tour. No one has been seriously injured here, but guests have reported things brushed against them. Just last week, a guest said his back was burning. When he lifted his shirt, I used the light on my phone to see. He had several, different-sized scratch marks on his back. Now, if you're ready, please follow me."

Alex held my right arm as we followed Patty along the hallway, into a large room. The lingering sunset glow in the sky and two surrounding street lights provided only enough light to see few details in the room. She turned her phone light off when she reached the middle of the room and turned around until the group was together again.

Alex gradually strengthened her grip on my arm. She darted her eyes all over the room.

"Alex, what's the matter?"

She looked at me, stone-faced and whispered, "He's here."

Chapter 18

Shadows

"How can you tell?"

She kept looking around the room.

"Alex, how can you tell?"

"I can feel him."

"Where is he?"

"I don't know. Somewhere in this building though. What the hell is he doing here? And how did he get here?"

Patty started again, "The layout here is really easy. There's a long hallway that extends the length of the building on each floor with rooms on either side. If you get separated, there are two stairwells in each wing. Listen for the voices of the groups to rejoin us."

She continued her story, "This room was one of the cafeterias. Mark and I both carry voice recorders throughout our tours. After each one, we turn the recorders over to our techy guys who sit and listen to them for hours. Here's what they captured from my recorder a month ago."

The group leaned closer when she played the recording. We heard Patty's voice first. *Before we keep going, does anybody have any questions?* Immediately, a small child laughed and said one word. *Play?*

I pulled Alex to the side with my arm and said, "We need to get to the back of the group so we can break away."

"I think that's a *really* bad idea. Toby, we don't know this place."

"You heard Patty, it's an easy floor plan and we'll be able to rejoin them with no one knowing we left."

I waited for her approval. She looked beyond me and all around the room.

"Alex, if he's here, maybe we can lose him and keep him here."

"That's just dumb, Toby. How did he get here in the first place? He can go anywhere he wants."

"We have to try. Besides, this isn't an investigation at all. It's a tour. We need to be able to communicate and it doesn't sound like they're going to give us the chance to do that."

The group was talking over each other, responding to the voice on the recorder when Patty started walking again. We didn't follow until the last of the group passed us. Our eyes adjusted to the dark and we could see inside doorways. My eyes were open wide to see as much as I could and looked into doorways on both sides of the corridor. When I saw a stairwell to the right, I got Alex's attention and she followed me until we were hidden from the rest of the group. I peered around the corner into the hallway and watched them walk away. Patty's voice faded. No one noticed we were missing.

"Alex, what did you feel when you said he was here?"

"Like you said, I can't explain it, I just know."

"Is the feeling any stronger now than it was before?"

"No."

"If it gets stronger, let me know. He could be close."

We turned to face the stairs and looked around before we took the first step. The walls were spray-painted with graffiti and the concrete floor was covered in dust and dirt. We walked up the first set of steps onto a landing, turned and climbed more to get to the second floor. I peered around the corner to look up and down the hallway to make sure the other group wasn't nearby.

"I think we're clear," I said.

We stepped into the long hallway and walked towards the end of the East Wing to our left. There was a large room, like the one on the first floor.

"Another cafeteria," I whispered when I noticed long, metal tables against the wall and a pass-through cutout where trays and dishes were sent to be washed. Alex covered her mouth when a foot-long rat ran out of the pass-through, along one of the metal tables and around a corner. There were paper wrappers and cups from modern-day fast-food places on the floor.

"Let's check out the rooms," Alex whispered.

We crept along the hall, looking into doorways. Each room was only ten feet square. Some rooms on the right had small window openings and others didn't. All the rooms on the left were open to the outside. I walked into one to get my bearings. When I could see out, I saw the thick woods, a few cars in a gravel lot and a golf cart.

"Toby."

"Yeah," I said as I turned around. Alex was looking at the floor in a corner of the room.

"Look."

I stepped closer to where she was pointing and saw distinct footprints from the soles of shoes on the gritty floor; shoes I estimated to be only five inches long. Alex said, "Maybe one of the employees brought their kid in here."

"I don't think so. Look. No prints leading into the room or out. They're only in the corner there."

We walked back into the hallway and continued towards the West Wing. Few rooms had anything of interest in them. The ones that did were littered with fast food trash, just like we saw in the cafeteria. Voices were audible from the far end of the hall.

"Shit! One of the groups is coming to this floor," I said. We ran down the hallway, looking both ways. The second that Patty came into sight from the farthest stairwell, Alex and I sidestepped into another one, closer to the center foyer. I looked up the steps of the stairwell, then down. I reached for Alex's hand and we started down the steps towards the first floor.

We darted across the hallway into a room on the front of the building in the West Wing. When our heartbeats slowed, I gazed around the room and sighed.

I whispered, "Is there anyone here with us?" We stood still, looked around without moving our bodies and listened for a response. Alex peeked out into the hallway and crossed into another room. She disappeared into the dark room and I could only hear her shoes shuffling on the floor until she asked, "Hi, my name is—Alexandra. Does anyone here want to talk? I sure could use a friend."

She shuffled her feet around the room occasionally. "Toby, come over here," she whispered. I walked across the hall. "I feel something in here. Is that what you're talking about?"

I felt it, too. A chill, but also a warmth. The entity wasn't malicious, it was calming.

Alex spoke again when the feeling was gone, "Thanks for coming to see me."

I turned and told her, "You're good at this."

"You said they need to trust us first."

"Yes," I said, smiling.

I turned to walk out of the room. My foot touched something. It was too late to stop the momentum of my stride. We jumped when we heard a ding at the same time as we heard, POP! Reactive, we looked down at the floor and saw a small box with a tiny crank and a clown face protruding from the top. We didn't move an inch; only listened, but didn't hear either of the groups. I kicked it to the side and said, "I hate those fucking things."

We peaked around the corner again before walking out, found another stairwell and started up the steps. I stopped at the second floor and listened. I heard Patty's voice on the other side of the closed door into the hallway, grabbed Alex's hand and led her up to the third floor.

"Toby."

She sounded frightened.

"Yes," I replied.

"He's close."

"How close?"

"Not right here, but we're getting closer to him. You can't feel it?"

"No, I can't."

The door to the third floor was open. Without hearing either group, we walked into the hallway near the far end of the East Wing and stood outside the doorway to the cafeteria. We looked through the openings to the large room with support columns scattered throughout.

"What's that?" Alex whispered.

"What do you see?"

She lifted her arm straight out in front of her and extended her index finger that pointed towards one of the columns. "Someone is hiding around that support."

I inched closer to her and looked to where she was pointing. I couldn't see him straight on, but as I scanned my eyes from left to right, there appeared to be a boy's head peeking from behind it.

"Do you want to talk?" Alex asked. "We're not going to hurt you. Can you talk to us?"

The shadow figure of the boy pulled his head behind the column and he ran to hide behind another.

"What's your name?" she asked.

He whispered, "Alex."

She chuckled, "That's my name, too. Alexandra."

"I'm just Alex," He said.

"Alex, I'm looking for a man who doesn't belong here; a stranger. Have you seen anyone?"

He ran and hid behind another post.

I spoke softly, "Alex, where is the stranger?"

He ran towards the opening in the front of the building and vanished. A door opened down the hallway and we heard Patty's voice.

"This is the third floor. We call this the shadow floor." The group walked towards us. We looked around for a place to hide, but not knowing where the tour was going next, we waited for them. A woman from the group spoke fast when she said, "Somebody's down there; towards the end of the hall."

"Dammit," I grumbled and stepped into the middle of the corridor. "Hi, Patty, it's us. Sorry about that. We were still looking in one of the rooms and lost the group."

"That's okay, come on over. You're in for a real treat."

We joined the others and Patty instructed, "Here is where I need you to turn the power off your phones. You'll need your eyes to adjust to the dark as much as possible."

Cell phone faces lit up and dimmed sporadically until everyone settled and Patty said, “I need a volunteer.” No one spoke.

“I’ll do it,” I said.

“You’re a brave man. You don’t know what you’re volunteering for.”

“I’m up for it; whatever it is.”

She addressed the group, “Like I said, we call this the shadow floor. Everyone, face this way and look towards the end of the hall of the West Wing. There’s a door at the end with a small square window on it. Can everyone see it? There’s barely any light coming through that window.”

Everyone confirmed they could see the window, then she turned to me, “What’s your name, sir?”

“Toby.”

“Where are you from?”

“Tennessee.”

“Toby, have you ever had any paranormal experiences?”

I was thankful for the darkness because she couldn’t see my expression. Alex, who was right behind me, laughed through her nose so the others couldn’t hear her.

“Um, a few I think,” I replied.

“You’re about to have another one,” she said. “Here’s what I want you to do. Walk down to the end of the hallway, right up to the window on that door. When you reach it, turn around and walk ten steps back towards us.”

With hard sole shoes on, I dramatically heel-toed along the hallway. The sound of my footsteps echoed off the bare walls.

Without Alex, emptiness washed over me as I walked towards the end of the hall. I no longer heard my group whispering to each other or moving at all. I turned around when I reached the end with the small window and started back towards the others. *One, two, three, four, five, six, seven, eight, nine—ten.* When I stopped, I stood with my feet shoulder width apart and looked down the hallway towards my group, but I couldn't see them. Shadows hid them. For the first time, I felt alone in that haunted building.

Patty asked me to shift so the others could see where I was. I heard faint gasps from the group and one person said, "Oh my God, can you see them?" Others joined in with whispered wonder.

"What do you see or feel?" she asked.

"It's weird," I said. "The opening to the outside is to my right, but I feel like my whole back is freezing from my head to my feet." I put my hands out to feel the air and continued, "but there's no breeze at all."

I stood there with the front of me feeling warm and my entire back feeling cold. One man in the group said, "Wow, look at all of them." The cold sensation left and my body temperature felt equal all around. I took a breath to explain, but a woman spoke first, "They just left him." I confirmed by saying, "Yeah, they're gone, aren't they?"

Patty instructed me to come back. When I returned, Alex asked, "What did you feel?"

"Like there were three or four entities behind me."

She looked down the hallway, then back to me and said, "That's how many we saw break away from you."

Patty announced, "That concludes our tour. I hope you enjoyed it. Come on back sometime. We offer overnight investigations, too."

Alex and I procrastinated until we were at the back of the group. When we reached the second floor, the door to the hallway was open. The others reached the landing between the first and second floors. I grabbed Alex's hand, pulled her to the side, and we stood with our backs to the wall until the stairway was silent. We climbed the stairs, back to the third floor and tiptoed through the doorway. Alex whispered, "Let's go back to the cafeteria."

We turned to walk to the end of the East Wing and heard from behind us, "Psst." The shadow boy stood in the middle of the hallway, only ten feet away from us and slowly pointed to the ceiling.

"Thank you, Alex," I said. "Thank you."

Chapter 19

Fourth Floor

The shadow boy ran down the hall and dissipated in front of us. Alex said, "Come on, let's go," and I followed her to the stairwell we had just come from. She ran up the steps. When she reached the landing and turned, she doubled over before her foot touched the next step to the fourth floor, then fell backwards and her back hit the wall.

"Alex!" I called.

"I'm okay."

"You sure as hell don't look okay; what happened?"

She was holding her ribs on her left side and said, "I feel like I got hit again, like it just happened."

I stood, facing her. "Are you okay?"

"Yeah, it's going away—that sucked."

"Let's stay here for a minute."

"NO!" she yelled. "I've had enough of that mother fucker. This ends tonight."

"Where is he?" I asked.

She looked up the stairs to the closed door with rage in her eyes. We were both trying to catch our breath when she pushed herself off the wall with her back and continued to glare up the stairwell.

"Alex."

Ignoring me, she took a step towards the stairs and dropped her hand away from her ribs. I followed as she took each step with a purpose. One by one, she climbed until she reached the landing and peered out the crack where the doors met. A street lamp cast a thin line of light that stretched her length. Dust swirled in the beam between the doors and Alex's body. She wrapped one finger at a time around the handle. The door opened with a long, high-pitched *creak* until it was open just enough for her to walk through. I held the door and followed her into the fourth-floor hallway with the light covering us from the street lamp across. Alex looked towards the East Wing, then the West. She closed her eyes and put her hand in the middle of her chest, took two deep breaths and sprinted to the right towards the West Wing.

The floor plan was different on the top level. I ran to catch up but she was too fast. I heard a noise behind me, like someone dropped a metal bar on the concrete floor. When I turned to look, there was nothing. I turned around to face the West Wing. Alex was gone. I crept along the corridor, regulating my breathing the best I could, and peered into each room. Past the light of the street lamp, the building was dark; darker than the other floors, it seemed.

"Alex," I whispered occasionally. I tiptoed into a tiny room on the left. "Are you here?" I peeked around the corner and stepped out of the room.

"Proooooteeeect Herrrrr."

The whisper seemed to echo off every wall. When it faded, I stood in the darkness.

Thud

I looked up at the ceiling.

"The roof," I whispered to myself.

I continued along the hallway and darted my eyes back and forth to scan the entire floor.

Tink

The sound came from down the hall in front of me. I sidestepped into a room on the right, leaned my shoulder on the wall and peered the length of each Wing.

"Where are you?" I whispered loudly.

Her voice scared the hell out of me. I gasped and jumped into the hallway. It came from behind me; from the very same room.

"I'm right here—beside you—as always."

Alex stepped into the corridor and smiled. She walked towards me, placed her hand on the side of my face, and kissed me.

She stepped backwards and tilted her head from side to side. She looked up at the ceiling and down towards the floor. She stretched her arms out to her sides and Sara's translucent body walked out of Alex.

Her calming eyes looked into mine and Alex stood, staring at her, confused until she said, "How? When?"

Sara turned around to face her, "Like I said, this ends tonight."

Alex looked around, still confused. Sara spoke again, "Thanks for the ride."

She jumped into the air and vanished. I stepped towards Alex and she said, "She must have done it last night when we were in bed. I felt it. I told her to get out and I thought she was gone."

"That's why you couldn't get warm," I added.

"And why I was so tired on the way here."

"Shit," I said. "That's why you could sense him. Do you feel his presence anymore?"

"No, I don't."

"Are you okay?"

"No, I'm not okay; I'm pissed."

I reached for her hand, "Good, come on."

We ran from room to room, looking for a stairway to the roof.

"Here," I said as I stepped through the open door. We climbed the first set of stairs to the roof and she called out, "Toby."

She had one foot on the landing and one still on the last step.

"What?"

"Let's get out of here."

"What do you mean?"

"Look, I don't know how *he* got here, but I brought her here."

"What are you saying?"

"Toby, they're out of your house. Let's get the hell out of here; let's get to the truck and take off."

I looked up at the rest of the stairwell.

This ends tonight. She's right. We could leave them here and go home. What if Sara needs us? I don't know what we could do, but if there is something, we should be there for her. She's not the elegant woman she pretends to be. It's her fight. It's her problem. Don't make it your business, Toby. If we leave her and she comes back, she could be as dangerous as Daryl.

"Come on," she urged.

"Alex, this has to stop—forever. If we leave now, we'll always wonder if they'll come back. I hate to point out the obvious, but that dream you had wasn't your dream at all. It was Sara's. I think Daryl's right; she's not the elegant woman she pretends to be. If she comes back, how will she act if we leave her? We *have* to see this through."

The door to the roof flew open and we both looked through the opening. Alex whispered, "We have to go."

"Alex, I know you're pissed and you have every right to be. I need to see this end."

With both of her hands on the railing, she looked down the center of the stairwell all the way to the ground floor. She shook her head and looked at me for a moment, then to the open door at the top of the steps.

"Alex, if shit gets as bad as before, we go. That's the backup plan. If we can stay hidden and see this end; I'll feel a whole lot better about going home."

I let her think about it without further convincing. She grinned and whispered, “I hate you, Tobias Miller,” and stepped up to the landing.

We reached the open doorway, peered around, and stepped out.

It was cold. There was little to block the strong breeze from the West. In front of us was a brick structure that resembled a security station. The rest of the roof was open on both wings, except the three-foot-tall retaining wall along the perimeter. A gargoyle towered above us.

Sara’s screaming voice shattered the silence, “Show yourself!”

We scanned the roof to the ends of each wing, but neither Sara nor Daryl were visible.

The night fell silent again.

“Where is she?” I whispered.

“It sounded like it came from over there.”

She pointed to the end of the East Wing.

“Come on,” I said, “Let’s get inside.”

We sprinted through the doorway to the guard station. There were four small rooms with arched brick doorways joining them.

Click. Click. Click. Click. Click.

The distinct sound of footsteps echoed from within the walls.

“Who’s there?” I said aloud.

Daryl’s deep, sinister laugh echoed off the walls, and he said, “Nice work, Tobias. You pulled through.”

“How do I know you’re going to keep your end of the deal?”

“I’m a man of my word. You’ll never see me again—once I exercise this bitch.”

“Daryl—”

"Shut up, Alex," he interrupted.

Her mouth sealed shut. She breathed fast through her nose between silent screams.

"Until a year-and-a-half ago, I never touched your precious sister, 'cept to protect myself."

He showed himself; as an apparition at first until he stood in front of us as if he were alive again. He slowly unbuttoned his flannel shirt, pulled it off his back and turned around. He had long scars across his chest, his stomach, his shoulders and his back, including a clean, two-inch scar on the back of his right shoulder.

Alex's muffled screams stopped, and she opened her mouth, "Daryl," she whispered.

He pulled his hands up to his head, separated his disheveled hair. "Also, here." He had another three-inch scar on the side of his head, behind his ear. "And here," he said as he turned again and dipped his head down so we could see. Another scar stretched through his scalp from his hairline to the crown of his head.

"Your sister's a violent woman when she's angry." He reached for the scar on his right shoulder. "This was when I caught her cheating on me the first time." He ran his finger along the length of the big one on his head. "And this, from the second time. I never stopped her from anything. On her nights out with you, I went out with the boys. When I sensed something wasn't right, I came home early, parked at the end of the drive by the trees and walked into the house. I couldn't believe what I was hearing. I crept through the house and she got louder, but I had to be sure. One of the doors to the bedroom was open a little. Even though I knew what I was hearing, I got to the doorway and peered through the crack in the door."

"Oh my God," Alex whispered.

"I pushed the door open without a sound, stood there with an unobstructed view and watched them as she moaned his name before I spoke. He was my best friend."

He pulled his shirt back on and buttoned it. "'I see how it is.' That's all I said. Everyone talks big about what they'd do if they ever caught their wife cheating on them. *Everyone* hasn't been there."

He looked at Alex with his blackened eyes and finished, "Your sister's fucking boyfriends were more important than you. That's why you never saw her."

"DARYL!" Sara screamed again. All three of us turned our gaze towards the sound on the end of the West Wing. Daryl turned back to Alex, pointed his finger in her face and said, "It's not over between me and you," and walked towards Sara.

She became visible as he stormed towards her. Wind blew. Sara's hair fluttered behind her. She put her arms out and screamed, blasting the air away from her in all directions. Daryl flew backwards off his feet as she laughed and the air calmed.

"You were right," I said. "Let's get out of here."

We ran out of the structure and towards the stairwell.

"Not so fast," Sara said when she appeared, blocking us.

Alex spoke first, "Is he telling the truth?"

Sara calmly lifted her hand to Alex's face, "Sissy."

"Don't touch me!" Alex scolded.

She put her hand down and stared with sad eyes; her body still tense. "Alex, you don't know what it's like."

"Shut up, Sara," she said. "You brought this upon yourself."

Sara's body relaxed and she sighed. "Alexandra."

Blackness engulfed us. I reached out for Alex's hand. "Don't let go," I said and dropped to the ground. "Come on."

I tried to crawl towards the stairwell, but the darkness, combined with things blowing around from the wind, made me dizzy. We seemed to crawl forever. I heard sounds of agony and pain from both Sara and Daryl, but neither of them were speaking.

"Where the hell is the stairwell?" Alex shouted.

"It was right in front of us," I yelled over the noise.

A yell came from somewhere behind us, "HEY!"

The wind stopped and the blackness faded.

We looked all over. We were in the open area in the middle roof over the East Wing. Daryl and Sara were on the ground near the entrance to the security station.

Daryl stood slowly, "Who the fuck are you?"

"I live here. You don't get to bring your petty bullshit into my house."

I turned around. He was a teenage boy with friction burns around his neck. I stepped towards him, "Jimmy?"

Daryl stepped forward, "Is he kidding me right now? This punk-ass kid has proposed a challenge."

"It's not a challenge. Get out and don't ever come back."

Daryl stood straight. A blackness spread from him again. I told Alex, "We need to get the hell out of here."

Jimmy suddenly appeared directly in front of Daryl and the darkness faded. "You don't know darkness, my friend."

Shadow figures walked towards him from every direction. Alex called out to Sara who floated next to us and Jimmy continued, "We've all spent time in solitary under the worst conditions you could imagine. I'm the only one who survived it; but I didn't survive the surviving."

He lifted his head and pointed to the rope burn around his neck. "You think you had it so bad. You think this lady here ruined you. She must be powerful to ruin you."

Daryl snapped, "She's nothing!"

"If she didn't ruin you, you did it to yourself."

"You don't know what—"

"Yes, I do," Jimmy interrupted. "I know what she did—and she'll answer for it. Maybe not today, but her time will come."

Jimmy slowly looked towards Sara with a grin and she vanished without a warning. The shadow people continued to close in on Daryl and he looked around as more appeared. His enraged, blackened eyes turned to me as he faded. Before disappearing, he shot straight into the air, as Sara did from the fourth floor. The shadow people scattered, and we ran to Jimmy.

"Thank you," I said. "I can never repay you."

"Not so fast," he said. "I didn't do it for you. You brought this into my house. Keep your fucking problems behind your front door.

He looked at Alex, "And you," he said. "I've spent countless sleepless nights in the pit, dosed with caffeine pills to reflect on what I did. Not only the fights I got into here, but I robbed my father and step-mom under my mother's direction, with help from my sister and a few friends. Who the hell are you to receive gratitude for murder?"

Jimmy looked at the ground and he said, "It's not payment I want."

He turned, walked towards the edge of the roof and put his arms out. Before he jumped, he said, "Everybody answers for their crimes, eventually." He lifted only his eyes, stared at Alex with an evil laugh, and stopped.

"Everybody."

Connect with me on social media for announcements of Book 3.

Acknowledgements

For Kris. Without you, this book wouldn't be what it is. So, what; we had to rewrite most of the book after 100 pages were already written. Your idea was genius.

Rob Williams at www.ilovemycover.com. I can't tell you how many times people have stopped to look at Book 1 because of the cover when they have no interest in paranormal. You have saved many sleepless nights, filled with nightmares for several visitors to bookstores and libraries.

To Laura Wilkinson. You are everything an author looks for in an editor, all wrapped up in one. Thank you.

Rick Lite at www.stressfreebookmarketing.com. You choose your clients wisely. Thank you for believing in The Ghost Between Us.

To my fans, especially my Dad, Skip, my Mother-in-Law, Maryann, my sister Bev, my son, Mychal, Marti Sholty, Jerry Nelson, Scott Walton, Tia Johnson, Mel Brown, and hundreds of social media fans who engage in my posts, share them and have truly been excited for me to finish Book 2.

About the Author

Pete Nunweiler is an emerging multi-genre author whose talent includes motivational self-development, a memoir and fiction. He has the keen ability to capture emotion in his writing through relatable characters and experiences.

He's able to do this successfully with more than fifteen years of leadership and leadership development, eighteen years of training experience and his core belief to try everything possible in life because you don't know what you're going to like.

Pete is a proud member of the Independent Book Publishers Association and originally from the village of Springville, NY, then Lititz, PA and currently resides in Indianapolis. He is married to his wife, Kris. Together, they are avid landscape photographers, specializing in waterfalls and cascades, primarily in The Great Smoky Mountains and the surrounding area. As a colorblind photographer, in 2014, along with Kris, they advanced their hobby into an online business under the name Nunweiler Photography. Their art can be found at www.nunweilerphotography.com.

Pete is an Eagle Scout from Troop 18 in the North Star District of the Crossroads of America Council of the Boy Scouts of America and continues to contribute to the Boy Scouts. In 1998, Pete was recognized as one of the top service providers in his company of 12,000 employees and considers that to be his greatest recognition. Pete is originally from the village of Springville, New York.

Other Books by Pete Nunweiler

The Ghost Between Us: – Book 1 of this Series

One Hundred Seventy Days – A Caregiver's Memoir of Cancer and Necrotizing Fasciitis.

The powerful true story of the unwavering strength of a woman and the indivisible bond of her family.

How Much Water Do We Have?: 5 Success Principles for Conquering any Challenge and Thriving in Times of Change

You'll learn how to find, acquire, and use the 5 Waters of Success – and how to share them with your team and family members. Are you thirsty? Dive in!

@5WatersBook, #5Waters

Published by Dave Burgess Consulting, Inc.

$14.95
ISBN 978-1-5323-7437-1
51495>
9 781532 374371

CPSIA information can be obtained
at www.ICGtesting.com
Printed in the USA
LVHW042001141022
730482LV00002B/15